Hot Witness

ALSO BY LYNN RAYE HARRIS

THE HOSTILE OPERATIONS TEAM SERIES:
Book 1: HOT Pursuit (Matt & Evie)
Book 2: HOT Mess (Sam & Georgie)
Book 3: HOT Package (Billy & Olivia)
Book 4: Dangerously HOT (Kev & Lucky)
Book 5: HOT Shot (Jack & Gina)
Book 6: HOT Rebel (Nick & Victoria)
Book 7: HOT Ice (Garrett & Grace)
Book 8: HOT & Bothered (Ryan & Emily)
Book 9: HOT Protector (Chase & Sophie)
Book 10: HOT Addiction (Dex) ~ Coming April 11, 2017
Book 11: HOT Valor (Mendez) ~ Coming July 18, 2017

HOT SEAL TEAM SERIES:
Book 1: HOT SEAL (Dane & Ivy)
Book 2: HOT SEAL Lover (Remy & Christina)
Book 3: HOT SEAL Rescue (Cody & Miranda)

Max: 7 Brides For 7 Brothers

Hot Witness
By Lynn Raye Harris

A MacKenzie Family Novella

Introduction by Liliana Hart

EVIL EYE
CONCEPTS

Hot Witness
A MacKenzie Family Novella
Copyright 2017 Lynn Raye Harris
ISBN: 978-1-942299-82-0

Introduction copyright 2017 Liliana Hart

Published by Evil Eye Concepts, Incorporated

ACKNOWLEDGMENTS

Thanks to Liliana Hart for asking me to be a part of her fabulous MacKenzie world! And thanks, as always, to my wonderful readers. You love HOT as much as I do, and I love bringing you news stories about the HOT world. Enjoy!

AN INTRODUCTION TO THE MACKENZIE FAMILY WORLD

Dear Readers,

I'm thrilled to announce the MacKenzie Family World is returning! I asked five of my favorite authors to create their own characters and put them into the world you all know and love. These amazing authors revisited Surrender, Montana, and through their imagination you'll get to meet new characters, while reuniting with some of your favorites.

These stories are hot, hot, hot and packed with action and adventure—exactly what you'd expect from a MacKenzie story. It was pure pleasure for me to read each and every one of them and see my world through someone else's eyes. They definitely did the series justice, and I hope you discover five new authors to put on your auto-buy list.

Make sure you check out Spies and Stilettos, a brand new, full-length MacKenzie novel written by me. This will be the final installment of the MacKenzie series, featuring Brady Scott and Elena Nayal. After eighteen books of my own and ten books written by other bestselling authors in the MacKenzie World, it's going to be difficult to say goodbye to a family I know as well as my own. Thank you for falling in love with the MacKenzies.

So grab a glass of wine, pour a bubble bath, and prepare to Surrender.

Love Always,
Liliana Hart

* * * *

Available now!

Spies & Stilettos by Liliana Hart
Trouble Maker by Liliana Hart
Rush by Robin Covington
Never Surrender by Kaylea Cross

Avenged by Jay Crownover
Bullet Proof by Avery Flynn
Delta: Rescue by Cristin Harber
Hot Witness by Lynn Raye Harris
Deep Trouble by Kimberly Kincaid
Wicked Hot by Gennita Low
Desire & Ice by Christopher Rice
Hollow Point by Lili St. Germain

CHAPTER ONE

As a member of the elite Hostile Operations Team, Jake "Harley" Ryan expected that deadly assignments were a part of the deal. What he didn't expect was to be sent on a suicide mission.

There were three men in the room besides him: Colonel John Mendez, the badass HOT commander; Lieutenant Colonel Alex Bishop, the quieter but no less lethal deputy commander; and Declan MacKenzie, the legendary founder and leader of MacKenzie Security, a firm with government contracts and operatives around the world. That a private contractor was here in the HOT command center didn't surprise Jake. That a private contractor was here to request *his* help did.

"You want me to go back to Georgia and pretend the last seven years didn't happen? Just waltz up to the clubhouse and act like nothing's changed?" He cocked his head as he stared at the three men. "What makes you think the Brothers will take me back? It's more likely they'll kill me on sight."

Declan MacKenzie exchanged a look with Mendez. Then he shoved himself off the table he'd been leaning against and reached for a folder. He took out a sheet of paper and handed it to Jake.

"They might kill you, sure," Declan said. "But I think you're smart enough not to let that happen. And the colonel here is smart enough to make sure you get sent home under less than honorable circumstances so everything looks legit. Play your cards right and they'll take you back."

Jake glanced at the paper in his hand—and his gut twisted. Judge Harold Mason, aged sixty-four, widely believed to be on the short list for a Supreme Court seat, lay in a coma in an Atlanta hospital after a single car crash. His wife had died. There was a picture of the accident scene. It wasn't pretty.

"That's the judge who offered you a choice, right?" Declan asked. "Prison or the military?"

"Yeah." It was more complicated than that, though. Judge Mason was responsible for who Jake had become—and who he hadn't become. Jake had been young and angry when he'd faced the judge. Hell, he'd even been stupid—but his court-appointed attorney had not. Jake had barely been eighteen, and he'd figured going down with the Brothers of Sin was simply a rite of passage. He was still a recruit at that point, but he'd have done anything to belong to that group of badasses and earn the right to be a full-fledged Brother.

His attorney, along with the judge, had convinced him otherwise—Jake still didn't quite know how—and here he was. An elite soldier. The best of the best. A man who could face overwhelming odds and win every time. Who stared death in the face and fucking laughed at it.

"He's still in danger," Declan said. "Unless we can get Brandon Cox and the Brothers on murder charges for Mrs. Mason and attempted charges for the judge."

Jake set the paper down. "Look, I'd do anything for Judge Mason. He saved my life—but I wasn't a witness to the crime. How can I possibly do anything to prove the Brothers had a hand in it?"

"You can't. But there's a woman who can."

Another piece of paper was thrust into Jake's hand. A woman's face stared back at him. She wasn't smiling. She had a faraway look that spoke of sadness and determination. She was climbing from a car, her long legs bared as her skirt rode up. She had long dark hair and blue eyes. She also had a wealth of tattoos, all in shades of black and gray—on her arms and legs, across her collarbone, over her belly where the cropped top she wore exposed the skin. There were words on her thighs.

It wasn't ugly, though. On her, it was beautiful. As if she were made to wear ink.

He shook himself. "Then why aren't you talking to her? Why ask me to get involved?"

It wasn't that he wouldn't throw himself on a grenade for the judge, but he wasn't quite seeing how this worked yet. Why they needed him.

"We'd love to talk to her—but she won't talk to us. Her name is Eva Gray. She's twenty-four, a tattoo artist. She does work for the Brothers. Hell, she may even be involved with one of them, though we don't know that for sure. But I can't get any of my guys close enough without putting her in danger. You, however, could walk in as a Brother and get what we need." Declan paused, his gray eyes growing troubled. "She's in danger too, Jake. If my FBI sources are right, she's the only witness willing to finger them. We have to get in there and get her out— and we have to convince her to talk or she'll never be safe again."

Jake glanced down at the photo. "She doesn't look worried. She's probably someone's old lady. Maybe even Brandon's. How do you know she'll talk at all?"

"She called in an anonymous tip to the FBI. She's willing but she needs some persuasion. Time is running out."

Jake stood and handed the photo back to Declan. This woman had dared to break the code and call in a tip. It might have been anonymous, but clearly the FBI knew who'd done it. And the Brothers had ways of finding out things they shouldn't know. When they did, they'd eliminate her.

"When do I go in?"

* * * *

Eva Gray shook her hair from her face and bent back to the arm of the biker she was currently tattooing. It was a colorful tattoo, one with skulls and roses and twining vines. The dude gritted his teeth as she set her needle to his skin again. The inside of the arm was one of the worst possible places to get a tattoo. The skin was thin, the nerve endings were abundant, and it hurt like a motherfucker.

"You gonna make it, Duke?"

The old bastard snorted. "Yeah, little girl, I'll make it."

Eva laughed as she continued her line work. "I think you will. Tough man."

She kind of liked Duke, as much as it was possible to like any of the Brothers. Which, for her, wasn't much. But he was nice enough and never tried to cop a feel the way the others did.

The door to the studio opened and a chill breeze rolled in. It was October, so the days were getting cooler, but that wasn't the source of the coolness in the room. At least not for her. Without looking up, she knew that Brandon Cox had walked in.

Easy, Eva.

Yeah, she had to take it easy. Because she'd gone through a lot to get this close to the Brothers—to Brandon—and it wasn't over yet. Years of work. No sense rushing when she was on the verge of victory. Patience was a virtue. It had served her well for seven long years of preparation, and it would continue to serve her well until she achieved her goal.

"Hey, baby, how you doing today?"

Eva glanced up at Brandon and gave him a sugary sweet smile, even though he made her stomach turn. "Just great, Brandon. How about you?"

He swaggered over and leered at her. He wouldn't touch her. Not yet, though she suspected his patience was beginning to wear thin on that score.

"I'm great, baby. Be even greater if you'd let me taste those sweet lips of yours."

Revulsion slid down her spine like rancid grease. But she smiled anyway. "Can't do that, man. You know I don't mix business and pleasure."

When she'd started tattooing the Brothers six months ago, she'd made it clear that if they wanted her art, they had to respect her rules—which had become doubly important when she moved to the compound a little over two months ago. Since she was damn good at what she did, they went along with it—other than the various attempts at copping a feel, which she always stamped down hard.

"Honey, there are other tattoo artists."

"But none as good as me."

Duke snorted. "She's got you there, boss."

"Yeah, yeah, all right. Shame to waste that body though."

"Is there something you wanted, Brandon?" she asked. "I've got another hour on Duke before I can get to you."

"Not me, baby." He turned and made a motion and another man walked inside. "Need you to do something for my man Jake."

Eva's heart skipped as her eyes met cool amber ones. Her jaw felt as if it had dropped to the floor. She swallowed.

Jake Ryan. Dear God. He'd been a Brother all those years ago when Heather was still alive. She knew it because, before he'd joined a motorcycle gang, he'd been in her high school. She'd spent hours staring at Jake from behind her glasses. Hours imagining pressing her mouth to his and tasting him. He'd been a bad boy, moody and just this side of delinquent, and she'd been oh so fascinated. Her and every other girl.

He hadn't made it through their senior year, however. At a certain point, he'd left school. She'd seen him around town in his cut, the jacket that proclaimed him a Brother. How he'd gotten a motorcycle she'd never known, but just seeing him rumble through town on his Harley had been enough to set her heart racing.

Her heart was hammering now, and not because he was gorgeous. She told herself that he wasn't going to recognize her. No one had. No one. Not the people she'd known in school, not her aunt who still lived in town, not a single person. She'd changed that much. Deliberately.

Who she'd been before was dead, and there was only Eva Gray in her place. It had to be that way.

But she still dropped her gaze from Jake's and focused on Duke's arm. She'd bobbled the line she was working, but she could fix it.

"All right, sure. What's he want?" she asked.

Brandon clapped Jake on the back. "He's going to need the Brothers of Sin freshened up. It's faded a bit since he left us for the military."

Military? She'd wondered where he was when she'd returned to town and he hadn't been in the club anymore. Thought maybe he'd gone to prison or something. So many of the Brothers rotated through the system like it was a revolving door that she didn't think he'd be any different.

And she certainly hadn't cared that she'd be taking him down along with the rest of them when the time came.

"Sure thing. Just have to finish Duke first."

"Take your time," Jake said. His voice was so unexpected that it hit her like a splash in an icy pool. Deep, resonant, filled with all that sexy promise she'd worshipped back in the day.

After Heather had gone inside the club, she was only allowed out with an escort. She'd visited Eva and their mother as often as she could, and sometimes Jake was the one tasked with accompanying her when she did. He wouldn't come inside the house, but when Eva took him a drink on the porch, he was nice to her.

"I intend to," she said. Because she couldn't afford softness with these men. They were predators. One whiff of weakness and they'd rip her throat out.

He snorted. "I see why you hired her," he said to Brandon. "Sexy and bitchy. She'd make a great old lady."

"Don't go gettin' any ideas," Brandon said gruffly. "Eva treats her body like it's a sacred temple or something. She won't fuck a Brother. Will you, baby?"

She didn't glance up. "Nope. I gotta stay true to my art."

"See? Crazy bitch, but she's good with the ink."

"Love you too, Brandon," she deadpanned.

One of these days she'd go too far, but for now the leader of the Brothers of Sin only laughed. Evil, murdering bastard.

"You let me know when you're ready for some real lovin', baby, and I'll give it to you good and hard."

Not if she gave it to him good and hard first. And she wasn't talking about sex.

CHAPTER TWO

Duke didn't last another hour. Jake hadn't expected he would anyway. The inside of the arm was tricky, and the man had already had a lot done that day. When he came strolling out into the yard, his face red with pain, Jake bit down a smart-assed remark.

He'd only been back inside for a few days now, and he still wasn't sure they trusted him. He hadn't been suicidal enough to stroll into the compound where the Brothers hung out and worked on cars—and other illegal shit they kept hidden—and announce his return. Instead, he'd shown up at The Island, a bar the Brothers frequented. It was inside their territory and off limits to other gangs, though there was a mixture of lowlifes who frequented the bar and did business with the Brothers.

He'd put on his cut, fired up his Harley, and drove right into their midst. Brandon had been waiting when he arrived, standing outside on the bar's long porch and glaring like a motherfucker at the guy who dared to ride into BoS territory, wearing the colors and pretending to be one of them.

But then Jake stepped off the bike and tipped his chin at Brandon with a cool, "Whassup, boss?"

Brandon strode down the steps, his face showing his disbelief as some of the other Brothers gathered around. Some he recognized. Others he did not.

"Jake Ryan? Fucking Jake Ryan?"

They'd circled each other warily, and then Brandon came in for the bro hug, slapping him on the back as he squeezed tight.

"What the fuck, dude?" Brandon had asked.

Jake shrugged. "I did my time in the military. I want to come home."

It could have gone worse, that's for sure. For now, Jake was in, his Special Ops career a source of pride for Brandon and the Brothers. No doubt they'd soon put him to the test, but he couldn't worry about that yet. Right now, he had to figure out what Eva Gray knew and keep her safe until he could get her out.

Jake strolled into the small studio where Eva had set up her machines. He'd been trained by the best of the best and he missed nothing. There was a bed behind a curtain and a hot plate on a counter. She lived as well as worked here, which was no surprise, considering how busy the Brothers kept her. With around eighty members, plus recruits and old ladies, she had plenty of work.

She had her back to him, cleaning her machines. "Have a seat. I'll be with you in a second."

He shrugged out of his cut and dragged his T-shirt over his head. The Brothers of Sin tattoo on his shoulder had faded over time. It wasn't a particularly good one. He'd planned to have it removed or covered but he'd been too busy to get around to it. Some things were more important than erasing tattoos. Especially when those tattoos reminded him how easily his life could have been so different.

He got in the chair and kicked back. His gaze dropped down her back, over her ass encased in tight jeans, down to her boots.

He wasn't surprised she was gorgeous. He'd seen the pictures.

But he was surprised that she wasn't an old lady by now. These dudes had to be salivating to make her theirs, so the fact she wasn't yet committed to anyone spoke volumes about her determination to focus on her art.

And yet that endangered her too, because if she really had witnessed the Brothers planning a hit on the judge, her life was forfeit the minute they decided to eliminate all the loose ends. She was fine for now because she was inside the compound and working—but if shit got real and the cops came calling, she was dead.

Or would have been if he wasn't here. Because he wasn't letting that happen. He hadn't spent the last seven years learning how to be a soldier, and then a badass black ops warrior in order to let a motherfucker like Brandon Cox get the best of him.

Eva turned around and strode briskly over to him. Her eyes were a cool blue, and her hair was a dark, lush brown with golden highlights. She was sexy as fuck, that's for sure. And she didn't look too pleased to see him. He found that notion odd, but it's what he felt in his gut.

"How long you been here, babe?"

Her eyes narrowed as she sat down and pulled her light in to look at his tattoo. "Long enough."

He let his gaze slide over the planes of her face, the set of her brow, and something tickled his memory. No idea what, because he wouldn't have forgotten a woman like this one.

"You remind me of someone." He didn't know where that had come from, but the instant he said it, her entire body stiffened. He'd gotten good at reading people in his line of work and what he read now was fear. Interesting.

Her eyes met his, though he sensed it wasn't an easy thing for her to do. "Try another line because that one won't work."

He shrugged it off with a laugh. "Can't blame a guy for trying."

Because he didn't want to rattle her when he was here to protect her. Even if she didn't know it yet.

"This thing's faded a bit. Not a great job to begin with, I'd say."

"Nope, not really."

"I can fix it, but it'll take some time. I need to do some sketches, figure how best to utilize what's already there. Maybe we can add some elements behind it, make it pop. A confederate flag, maybe."

The idea of adding to the tattoo and making it even more prominent did not appeal. "No flags."

"All right, so we'll do a skull or something. It's your arm and your dime."

"How about we just pretty up what's there and not worry about flags and skulls and shit?"

Her lips flattened in annoyance. "Like I said, your arm."

The door burst open and Eva let out a little scream. Jake was on his feet in a split second, weapon drawn, protecting the woman behind him.

Brandon Cox's gaze flicked between them and his eyes narrowed. "Sorry, dude, but we've got a job to do. Need those special skills of yours. No time for tattoos."

Jake holstered the weapon and strode toward the door. "Then let's go."

* * * *

The party was in full swing in the yard. Eva peered out the door of her shop and looked at the bonfire flaring high in the center of the compound. The Brothers were drinking and yelling and doing all the wild shit they usually did during parties. The women were there too, of course. Hell, during parties like this, it wasn't unusual to find a biker with a woman wrapped around him as he pressed her against a wall and fucked her out in the open.

Eva blinked and shook her head and wondered yet again how Heather could have gotten involved with Brandon Cox in the first place. Heather had been a good girl, a cheerleader and a regular Sunday school attendee—and then she'd changed after high school, said she'd met a man and she was in love. The first time she'd come home on the back of Brandon's bike, Mama had been horrified. So had Eva.

Eva had been seventeen to Heather's twenty then, and she'd been so naïve. A man covered in tattoos, bearded, packing heat, and looking meaner than a cornered snake had not been what she'd expected her sister to fall for. Eva hadn't liked Brandon on sight.

Unfortunately, she'd been right. She fisted the curtain she was holding and dropped it. She didn't need to see what was going on out there. Earlier, when Brandon had come for Jake, they'd strode out into the yard and mounted up. Twenty-some odd Brothers had roared out of the compound, and she'd known they were up to no good.

Her gut had twisted at the idea of Jake being involved—but why did she even care? He'd been in the military and he'd come back. If he came back to the Brothers of Sin, knowing what they were, he was no better than they were.

But there'd been that moment when he'd said she seemed familiar and she'd nearly gasped. He'd rattled her. She couldn't afford to get rattled. She was on the inside after years of work—first to change her life and grow her art in a direction she'd never thought of before, then to get into this biker life and make it seem like she fit in.

She did not fit in. These people horrified her, but she would do anything to prove that Brandon had murdered Heather. When her sister's body was found on Christmas day seven years ago, the back of her head bashed in and bruises all over her skin, Eva had expected Brandon would be arrested soon after.

He had been, but it hadn't stuck. He'd had an alibi, but she had no doubt the Brothers had lied for him. They stuck together no matter what. Had Jake lied for him too?

There was a knock on her door and her heart kicked up. She went over to the door and shifted the blind. Jake Ryan stood on the other side, and her belly tightened in response.

She unlocked the door against her better judgement and opened it a crack. "What do you want? Shop's closed for the night."

He held up a plate with BBQ pork on it. "Thought you might want something to eat."

She let her gaze slide behind him, scanning the crowd. "Brandon won't like it if I let you in."

"Brandon is fucking his old lady in his room. He won't know." He turned and threw a look over his shoulder. "They're too drunk and too happy to run tell him."

Eva knew she shouldn't do it, but she opened the door so he could slip inside. She closed it quickly, locked it, and turned around, asking herself why in the hell she'd just done that. Why let him in? He was one of them and that made him the enemy.

He'd been here when Heather was killed. That didn't mean he knew anything…but what if he did? What if he'd been involved somehow?

She walked over and took the plate from him. "Thanks," she

said as she sat down on one of the stools by her drawing table and took a bite of pork.

"You could have come out and got some, you know."

"I don't mix with the Brothers when they're partying like that. Less chance of any misunderstandings."

"Meaning while drunk they're likely to forget your rules, huh?"

"Exactly."

"Yet you just let me in. What if I forget your rules?"

She reached under the table and pulled out a loaded .45. "I think I can handle one on one."

He laughed, and she tried not to like the sound. "You'd be surprised, Eva. But the truth is you're safe with me. I'm not one of them."

Her heartbeat sped up and her fork hovered in midair. "What does that mean?"

He sat in the client's chair and kicked his legs back, crossing them at his ankles. He smelled vaguely of leather and woodsmoke, and he looked almost clean-cut compared to the men outside that door. His hair was still short, for one thing, cut in a military style. And he didn't sport many tattoos at all. Certainly nothing on his hands, which she knew was likely due to military rules.

He had the beginnings of a beard, but the scruff on him was sexy. She kind of hoped he kept it the way it was now instead of letting it grow longer. And then she thought she really didn't care. Jake Ryan wasn't her type anymore, if he ever had been. He wasn't safe, and she intended to find a safe man when she finally had her life back again.

"It means I'm here because I was sent."

"Sent for what?"

"For you."

CHAPTER THREE

She grabbed her pistol and whipped it up to point at him. Jake didn't flinch. She wasn't going to shoot him. Not yet anyway. For one thing, it would bring what she least wanted: armed Brothers banging on her door. For another, she was smart and she'd want to know what he meant before she blindly pulled any triggers.

Her blue eyes flashed fire and the tattoos on her skin made her look seriously badass. Yet the gun trembled ever so slightly, as if she was not as confident as she seemed.

He studied her face, the planes and angles—and he knew he'd seen it before. He just didn't know where. Or when. Maybe he'd known her when he'd lived in town before. Obviously not tatted up the way she was now—and maybe with different hair, too. It was an intriguing notion.

"Who sent you?"

"Declan MacKenzie."

She swallowed. "I don't know who that is."

"I think you do. Even if you haven't met him before, you know who he is. You've heard the name."

"I hear a lot of names."

He leaned forward, staring hard at her. Hoping she got the message. "You're in danger here, Eva. You're a loose end. You know too much and Brandon isn't going to let you live just because he likes your art."

"I don't know anything."

"Who called in the tip on Judge Mason?"

She couldn't hide the way her face drained of color, or the way the gun wavered for a second. He could disarm her. Probably should. But he didn't move. He let her process it.

"You're a Brother. You've been a Brother since you were eighteen."

A sharpness pierced his gut. "How would you know that?"

Her eyes were wider than before. The gun dropped to her side and she lowered her head. "I just do. You're one of them. You came back. Brandon said so today."

"I came back for you, Eva. And because Judge Mason saved my life."

She shook her head. "I can't leave here. I can't."

He got up and went over to her, put a hand on her arm. His skin tingled at the touch, but he didn't draw back. She was lovely. It was no surprise he was attracted to her. And yet he felt something else too. It was a flame inside him. Not just a sexual flame, but one that spoke of warmth and belonging as well. Things he hadn't ever felt before. Not the kind of belonging where you loved your job and knew it was the only one for you. The human kind. The kind you felt with another person.

"You can't stay either. It's dangerous."

She tossed her hair defiantly. He dropped his hand away, but his fingers still itched to touch her. "In case you haven't noticed," she said, "this is a biker compound. You don't just waltz out when you feel like it. And if you think Brandon's not going to do anything if you roll out of here with me on the back of your bike, then you're wrong."

That much was true, but he'd deal with it when the time came.

"Why are you here? You don't like these guys."

"Of course I like them. They pay me."

He didn't believe her. He recognized contempt when he saw it, and she had it in spades. "You've been calling the FBI."

She swallowed. "Not me. No idea what you're talking about."

He stepped back and sank onto the chair again. But he didn't lean back. Outside, the party was in full swing. It was loud, with music and talk and the revving of engines from time to time.

"You used your own phone. Dangerous, but also probably the best option unless you can get into town and find a pay phone somewhere."

She put the gun back where she'd gotten it from. He took that as a good sign. Then she closed her eyes and leaned back in her chair for a second. When she opened them, her gaze was cool and clear.

"I overheard some things about Judge Mason, yes. The Brothers sit in my chair and talk like I'm not here, but I listen. Brandon's nephew is on trial for attempted murder in Atlanta, in case you weren't aware, and Judge Mason was the presiding judge. He'd already made some rulings in the case that were unfavorable—so Brandon got the idea that it was time for Mason to go. Brandon talked about hiring someone to install malware into the judge's car. This guy was supposed to program it to cut the power to the brakes once the car reached a certain speed."

"So who's the guy? Do you know?"

She shook her head. "I don't, not really. All I heard was the name Snake. A hacker of some sort, I imagine. Any hackers turn up dead lately?"

She said it half-jokingly, but he knew she wasn't joking at all.

"I don't know. I'll have to ask Declan to check it out. Is there anything else you can think of?"

She shrugged. "I don't know anything for certain. All I know is Judge Mason had a car accident and Brandon had talked about making it happen. I can't prove it. It could just be a coincidence."

"But you called the FBI."

She twisted her fork in the food but didn't eat anything else. "Because I believe he did it. I can't prove it, but I believe it. It's just my word against his—against all of theirs, because none of the Brothers will admit it's true. They stick together no matter what."

She sounded bitter.

"So tell me again why you're here, Eva. Why do you stay?"

"I have my reasons."

He sat back again, studying her. There was definitely something about her that tickled his memory. But what?

"If I were to ask the MacKenzies to dig into Eva Gray's background, what would they find?"

Her gaze was cool. "You tell me."

"I think they wouldn't find much of anything."

"Not worth the trouble then, huh?"

He stood. He'd been here long enough. It was time to get back to the party before Brandon missed him.

"Probably not, sugar." He started toward the door, but stopped and turned back to her.

Then he hauled her up into his arms and kissed her.

* * * *

Eva's heart beat like a wild thing. Her fingers curled into Jake's cut and her mouth, after the initial shock, slipped open. His tongue found hers, slid against it, encouraged her to kiss him back.

She did. Ravenously. In the back of her head, she kept telling herself this had to stop, that she did *not* need to encourage him. It was crazy to encourage him. Not to mention she had no clue what to do with him if she did.

But he tasted so good, a little like beer, a little like mint. His body against hers was hard and big, but he didn't scare her. He should because he was a badass biker and she didn't like that type, but he didn't.

She was still processing what he'd told her about coming here for her. He hadn't figured out who she really was, which was probably a good thing. If he knew she was Heather Collier's little sister—the shy, plump, mousy little sister who'd smiled shyly at him and mooned over him when he'd been in her class—well, he wouldn't be kissing her like this, that's for sure.

But he was kissing her and even though she should make him stop—because she didn't like bikers and never would—she told herself she could enjoy it for just a few more moments. She could pretend this was still high school and sexy Jake Ryan had noticed her, of all people.

He put a broad hand on her hip and tugged her in close—and she gasped at the evidence of his arousal. It also sent a thrill of shock and apprehension through her. She was not prepared to deal with this, and certainly not right here in the middle of one of the Brothers of Sin's bacchanalias. And if Brandon found out? Dear God. She didn't like to think what that meant for her, or for Jake.

Jake's fingers squeezed her hip, the other hand he'd threaded into her hair tightened—and then he let her go. Just like that, he pushed her gently away and stepped back. She zeroed in on his mouth—that beautiful, sexy mouth—and felt her heart sting that it was over while confusion rolled through her.

"Gotta go, Eva. But damn, girl, I wish I could stay."

He strode over to the door, unlocked it, and jerked it open before she could manage to find her voice.

All these years she'd protected herself, protected her heart and her body, treating her life like it was an instrument designed for one purpose: revenge. Yet a single kiss from a sexy biker, of all the damn things, had her tied up in knots, had her wishing that everything could be different.

But it couldn't. She was here to bring down the Brothers, here to ruin Brandon Cox—and she couldn't let anything or anyone stop her. Not even Jake Ryan.

"Me too," she finally whispered to the empty room.

CHAPTER FOUR

"Where you been?"

Jake looked up as Brandon strode into the yard at the same time he did. Brandon tugged on his fly, as if to make sure it was up, and grabbed a beer from someone as he strutted over. Jake didn't bother to lie. It was obvious he'd just come from the direction of Eva's shop.

"Checking with the tattoo chick on getting this thing done. She wasn't out here so I figured she'd be willing to work. She wasn't."

Brandon snorted as he took a pull from the beer. He swallowed and wiped his lips on his sleeve. "That bitch isn't willing to do a lot of things. But I tell you one thing, she's gonna suck my dick before too much longer. Because I've had just about enough of her prissy shit. Bitch thinks because she can work the ink like nobody else that she can call the shots like she owns the fucking place."

"Fuck that," Jake said, even though his heartbeat accelerated for a moment. He'd wiped his mouth when he'd left Eva's room. He could only hope he'd removed all traces of that dark wine lipstick she'd been wearing.

As if on cue, Brandon's gaze narrowed. It was dark in the yard now but the fire was blazing and the light from it illuminated their faces.

"Find you a woman, Jake?"

Jake shrugged. No sense lying about it. "I tried to kiss her. She slapped the shit out of me."

Brandon guffawed. "Sounds like Eva." He tipped the neck of his bottle toward Jake. "But don't do it again. Anyone gets to taste that bitch, it's gonna be me."

"Got it, boss."

He didn't like the way Brandon fixated on Eva. It wasn't a good thing at all. Jake remembered that Brandon used to slap his women around a bit, and Jake didn't think the dude had changed. A wave of revulsion washed over him. Why the fuck had he ever thought he'd belonged here with these people? They were so opposed to everything he believed that he couldn't imagine how he'd ever wanted to be one of them.

Because they were cool. Because you had nothing to look forward to back then.

Yeah, but still. Brandon Cox was a motherfucker who deserved to have his balls sliced off and fed to him, and yet he managed to stay out of prison and in business anyway.

Take tonight, for instance. A turf war over hookers and blow. Another gang thought they could come into BoS territory and pinch some of their suppliers. Brandon had responded with violent force.

"Man, you were indispensable tonight," Brandon said. "If I'd known the military could be so fucking good, I'd have sent some of the guys to the army to learn a few things. Those skills of yours are off the hook, man."

He clapped Jake on the back. Jake grinned, even though he'd rather use his skills on this man. "Yeah, handy shit they taught me in the Rangers."

The Rangers had only been the beginning, of course. He'd worked his way into Delta Force, which wasn't an easy thing to do, and then onward to HOT. He wasn't just a soldier. He was an elite special operator with the best fucking top secret outfit the United States had.

"Think you can show some of the guys how you disarmed four men before they could get the jump on you?"

"Yeah, sure. But let's do it when they're sober."

Brandon turned his head to look at the men and women partying down in the yard. Then he laughed and tossed back his beer. "Good plan."

He slung an arm around Jake's neck and hauled him toward a group of women. "Let's get you laid tonight. You deserve it."

It was the last thing in the world he wanted when his senses still reeled from kissing Eva Gray. He shot a glance to her window, wondering if she was watching. The curtain twitched and he knew she'd been looking at him. He wanted to charge back in there and take her in his arms again, but it was too dangerous— especially now that Brandon had told him Eva was off limits.

Brandon might have been patient with her thus far, but his patience was clearly running out. One wrong move, and Eva could end up dead.

And so could Jake.

* * * *

"Eva Gray," Declan MacKenzie said. "There's no record of her existence before about four years ago."

Jake frowned. He was standing at the edge of the compound,

on his phone, smoking a cigarette even though he'd given them up years ago, and watching the action around the fire. The party was winding down, with most everyone drunk or high or sleeping. Jake was still awake because while he'd had a few drinks, he hadn't had nearly as much as they'd thought he'd had—and he definitely hadn't taken any of the women to his room.

As soon as he'd been able, he'd walked out here away from the gathering and returned Declan's call. Jake had sent a text earlier asking about Eva, which he'd promptly erased. Declan knew to call him back rather than text him because it was safer that way.

Though Declan had told Jake to call him anytime, he still had a notion that he'd phoned at a bad time. There'd been the sound of a woman moaning in the background for a few moments when he'd first called. Jake could imagine exactly which woman it was, too. He'd met Declan's beautiful wife Sophia briefly when he'd gone to Surrender, Montana, in order to do his in-briefing with the MacKenzies before heading to Georgia.

"Eva looks familiar to me. I'm not sure why."

He heard the rustling of papers. "Does the name Evelyn Collier mean anything to you?"

Jake frowned. "Collier? Jesus."

"I take that as a yes."

He shoved a hand through his hair and kept an eye on the group of bikers. He couldn't afford to be overheard out here, and yet he was reeling as if he'd been clubbed over the head with a mallet. Evelyn Collier? He could hardly reconcile the chubby teenager he remembered with the sleek beauty of Eva Gray, and yet now that he'd heard the name, he knew it was the truth. Eva was Evelyn.

"How long have you known this?"

"Just got the info tonight. It took time to dig up. She was very thorough at covering her tracks."

"She had a sister."

"Heather. She was murdered seven years ago. Her body was found in a shallow grave, and she was beat up pretty badly."

Anger rolled through him fast and hard as the shape of what was going on here began to form. "She was Brandon's old lady."

"He was arrested, but the charges were dropped. They couldn't pin it on him. He said that she left him after a fight over another woman. Said she walked out of the compound alone, which witnesses corroborated."

"Of course they did." Because the Brothers lied for each other.

"The defense attorney suggested she'd been picked up by a motorist and killed after she'd left the Brothers of Sin."

"I remember. I wasn't here when it happened though. I was in jail, waiting for my attorney and Judge Mason to work something out. Once I took the deal, I never returned to the compound. I didn't see Brandon again."

"Do you think he did it?"

Jake clenched his jaw tight for a second. He remembered the way Brandon had been with Heather. She'd been unlike most old ladies, so delicate and out of place here—or so it had seemed. She and Brandon had fought like cats and dogs. Jake had witnessed Brandon hit her at least once. Maybe twice. Guilt and anger swelled in his gut. What a fucking asshole he'd been not to intervene. Not to kick Brandon's ass from one end of Georgia to the other. In spite of the fact it would have most likely gotten him killed, he should have done it anyway.

"Probably."

"And Evelyn Collier is inside that compound, calling herself

Eva Gray."

"Fuck."

"Yeah."

She'd told him she couldn't leave just yet, that she was waiting for something. He hadn't known what. He still didn't know what, but he was beginning to think it wasn't a good thing. Of course she'd called the FBI on the Brothers. But what else did she want? Something, because she wasn't running away.

A sick feeling swirled in his belly.

"What about Snake? Did you find anyone calling himself that?"

"Not yet, but we will. Cypher knows everyone who's anyone in the tech world. We'll find the guy."

"You need to call HOT. The colonel has connections."

"Already taken care of." There was a moment of silence before Declan spoke again. "Extract her as soon as possible. She can't stay much longer. If Judge Mason takes a turn for the worse...well, all hell's gonna break loose because the FBI will come calling. Once they do, once Cox knows someone left a tip—it won't take him long to figure out who it was."

"No, I don't think it will either." He dropped the cigarette and stubbed it out with his toe. "I'll get her out of here in two days' time. I'm going to need a place to go when I do."

"I'll send you the coordinates to a safe house. Memorize and delete."

"Copy that. Over and out."

CHAPTER FIVE

"What's your game, Eva?"

Her heart leapt in her throat at the sexy voice coming from behind her. She'd heard the door to her shop open, but she'd been cleaning her machines and she hadn't bothered to look at who it was. Not an easy task, but she'd had to learn to fake nonchalance a long time ago if she was going to fit in with the Brothers.

Now, she turned slowly in her chair and faced the man in leathers standing just inside her shop. Goddamn he was sexy. Tall, dirty blond hair, muscled. He had what looked like three days' worth of scruff and his eyes were slightly bloodshot. There were lines at the corners of those eyes. She hadn't noticed that yesterday. He looked like a commando rather than a biker at the moment.

She didn't like bikers *or* commandos. She didn't like dangerous men, and this one certainly was. She shivered as she thought of what he'd told her last night. He was here for her. Here to take her away before she'd accomplished her goals. She couldn't let that happen.

She'd tossed and turned for hours, wondering why he'd admitted he wasn't really one of the Brothers anymore. But she knew exactly why. She wouldn't rat him out to Brandon, because if she did that she'd be implicating herself—and Jake knew it. If she had to throw herself on anyone's mercy, it would be this man's before it would ever be Brandon's.

"Game? Sorry, I don't do games. You want me to work on your tattoo or what?"

He came over to her chair and shrugged out of his cut and then reached down and pulled his shirt up and over his head with one hand. She blinked as her mouth went dry. Oh dear God.

His belly was ridged with muscle, and his chest was broad and tanned. She'd seen it all yesterday when he'd done the same thing, but she hadn't let her eyes settle in any one spot then. She'd focused on his shoulder and the faded tattoo and ignored the rest.

She wasn't capable of ignoring it now, not when there were little sparks of sensation zinging through her body or when her feminine core started aching with need.

"Yeah, you can work on it. But you're also going to tell me what's going on with you…Evelyn."

Her insides turned to ice. She was vaguely aware that she was gaping at him, the needle in her hand suspended in midair, her muscles solidifying as if ice were creeping over her skin and making it happen.

How could he know? How? She'd been so careful, so methodical.

Eva swallowed and told herself to calm down. Told herself he was guessing. He didn't know anything. He'd thrown it out there to rattle her, that's all. It was a wild guess, though a good one. She could deflect it though. Of course she could.

"Nice guess, but Eva isn't short for anything."

His gaze met hers, and her breath caught. "I know who you are, Evelyn. I know why you're here."

Her hands were trembling. She could feel it, could see the needle shaking as she held it high. She set it down carefully and tucked her hands between her knees.

"You really don't. You don't know anything."

"You want to get him. You want him to pay for what he did to your sister. But how? How are you going to make that happen? You want to kill him?"

She could feel the blood rushing to her face. Of course she wanted to kill him. But she wasn't brave enough, dammit. Not yet anyway.

"I imagine a lot of people want to kill Brandon Cox. No one has done it yet, though."

"You've been inside for a couple months now. Why haven't you shot him with that .45 while he was at your mercy in this chair? Don't tell me you couldn't have."

She dropped her head, her eyes blurring. Yeah, she could have. A few times. "Because they'd have killed me if I did. And nothing would change other than he'd be dead, I'd be dead, and they'd have a new leader. There'd be no justice."

"So hanging out here and calling the FBI with anonymous tips was your plan?"

She swallowed. She could deny everything, deny she was Evelyn Collier and that Heather was her sister. But, dammit, she didn't want to. For once, she wanted *someone* to know. Besides, even if she denied it, she knew he wouldn't believe her. It was clear he knew the truth. Somehow, in spite of all her planning, he knew.

"I want to bring them down. All of them. And I want him to admit what he did."

She heard him sigh and she looked up, met those whisky-smooth eyes of his. "Tall order."

"Maybe so. But I'll find a way."

"Judge Mason's wife died in that crash. I think that's enough to get them if you testify about what you heard."

Fear rolled through her, followed by doubt. "It's not enough," she spat. "They'll find a way out of it. They always do."

"So what's the plan then, Evelyn? How are you going to take them down?"

"Stop calling me that," she growled. "I'm Eva. Evelyn died seven years ago."

"You were a sweet little thing," he said softly, and a shiver slid down her spine.

"You don't remember me, Jake Ryan. Don't pretend like you do."

He reached out and took one of her hands, gently pried it from between her legs. "I remember. You were in my English class. Mrs. Hamrick, fourth period. And you used to bring me drinks whenever I escorted Heather home for a visit."

"You brought her home three or four times. For all you know, I was trying to poison you so I could free her from the Brothers."

He snorted, and warmth blossomed inside. "I could completely believe that about Eva. Evelyn not so much."

She extracted her hand, mostly because of the heat prickling her skin. She didn't know what to do with him. What to do *about* him. He wasn't one of them, but he still wasn't the kind of man she could get involved with. Ever.

Another thought formed in her mind, chilling her. What if he *was* one of them and he was just getting her confession before turning her over to Brandon? It was exactly the kind of sick game Brandon would play.

"Hey," he said, and she met his gaze. He looked calm and

cool. "I can almost read your mind, beautiful. You're wondering if this is a setup, if the game is over."

"It's occurred to me."

"It's not a setup…but the game is definitely over."

* * * *

Her eyes hardened, turning icy blue. Her jaw tightened. He could see her fighting with herself, but what she hadn't realized yet was that she'd already lost. He wasn't letting her stay.

"I'll say when it's over, thank you. You don't get to tell me what to do. You know nothing of what I've been through, or what I'm willing to go through in order to win this battle. Nothing."

The last word was hard and bitter. He understood being driven by ghosts, but he also knew that you never outran them. He'd been trying for the last seven years. He was proud of who he'd become—but he wasn't proud of who he'd been.

"Brandon's ready to walk in here and force you to your knees, Eva. He's tired of you holding out on him. What are you gonna do then?"

She blinked and he could see the fear in her eyes. But then her jaw tightened and anger flashed over her face. "I guess I'll have to shoot him after all."

"There's a better way. We get the fuck out of here and you testify about what you heard—and anything else you know about the Brothers and their operations. The MacKenzies will follow the trail and get the evidence to back you up."

"You don't know that."

"I do." Because the MacKenzies would also be working with the Hostile Operations Team. Not that he could tell her that, of course, but what the MacKenzies couldn't find, HOT could, because it had the kind of access few organizations could boast.

Hell, the president's son-in-law was HOT. Shit got done when HOT got involved.

Her eyes were glittering. "Where were you when Heather was killed? Did you see him hit her? Threaten her?"

His gut was a knot of anger and guilt. But he wouldn't lie to her. "Yeah, I saw him slap her around sometimes. I'm not proud of that, but I was eighteen and that's how it worked in the Brothers. Old ladies knew their place—and when they got out of line, they got knocked back into it."

A lone tear slid down her cheek and his heart twisted in sympathy. "That's fucking disgusting."

"It is. But I'm sure you've seen your share since you've been here."

"A little."

"I was in jail when your sister disappeared. Breaking and entering. Theft should have been on there too, but my attorney got that one thrown out. And then I met Judge Mason and everything changed." Jake sucked in a breath. "He saw something in me, I guess. He saved my life. I couldn't save your sister—but I'm damn sure gonna save you."

She sniffed and crossed her arms. "So what's the deal? You just think we're gonna stroll out of here or what? You know that won't happen. You know the Brothers won't let it. You just came back. They might have welcomed you home with open arms, but they won't let you leave without someone shadowing your every move. Brandon may play nice with you, but he doesn't trust you, I promise you that."

"I know he doesn't. So when we break out of here, it's for real. No strolling, no joyriding. We're going through the fence, and we're going tonight."

Her eyes widened. "You're crazy! Even if I agreed to go, how do you expect us to get away with that? There's nothing but woods out there for miles. Besides, I won't leave my machines and my portfolio."

"Are they worth your life?"

She swallowed. "No, of course not. All I'm saying is I don't think this is the way."

"You got a better plan?"

She didn't answer, and he nodded. "Then we go tonight, and you can leave the machines. They're replaceable."

"I'm not ready to leave just yet."

"Judge Mason is hanging on by a thread. If he dies, the FBI is storming this place—and when they do, Brandon's gonna know someone betrayed him. Who do you think he's going to blame?"

Her lip quivered. "You're the new guy. You tell me."

He snorted. "Nice try, Eva, but it's gonna be you. I'm not the one who was here when they were still making plans. They'll question him, but without real evidence to go on, they'll have to let him go. And when they do, he's going to be tying up the loose ends. You feeling me?"

"Yes." The word was clipped, but she got the point he was making.

"Good. Now you planning to do anything about this tattoo or what? If I walk out of here with no work done for the third time, Brandon's gonna start asking questions."

She rose and went over to get her drawing. "This is what I planned," she said, turning it toward him. She'd completely redrawn the Brothers of Sin. He'd told her no skulls, but of course she hadn't listened. The skull fit the logo and would help cover up the worst of the old lines on the tattoo.

"Fine. But only if you add a rose."

She blinked. "What for?"

"For you."

She shook her head. It wasn't a shake of denial so much as a gesture of disbelief. "You're crazy."

"Sometimes. But if I've gotta wear this tattoo that reminds me of when I was a fucking piece of shit, I want some of you in it." He looked pointedly at the roses on her sleeves. Clearly, she liked roses.

She reached for her pen and set the page down on her drafting table. Her fingers trembled as she hovered over the drawing—and then she touched the pen to paper and all traces of her agitation seemed to disappear.

"I'd have never thought you'd end up as a tattoo artist," he said softly after they hadn't spoken for a few moments. "Not at all the vibe you gave in high school."

She snorted. "No, I wanted to be an interior designer. But that was before Heather died."

He couldn't help but be astonished over her transformation from the shy girl in high school to a sexy, tattooed ballbuster. This woman didn't take shit from anyone.

"You did all of this to get close to the Brothers. You changed everything about yourself, and you covered your body in ink."

She shrugged. "You do what you have to in war, right?"

He felt the truth of that comment all the way to his core. "Yeah, you do."

She held up the paper. "How's this?"

His gaze slipped over it, but what really drew him was her. Her blue eyes, the brown hair with golden tips, and the dark lipstick and eyeliner. Her jaw was angular and slightly prominent, but it didn't detract from her beauty. She looked cool and determined, and his admiration for her notched up.

"Beautiful," he said. But he wasn't talking about the tattoo.

CHAPTER SIX

It was dark by the time Eva was finished tattooing for the day. She glanced at her phone. It was only seven o'clock. She hadn't heard from Jake since she'd finished working on him earlier.

He hadn't said another word about his plan because several of the Brothers had come into the shop and hung out shortly after she'd started working on him. She'd pretended not to care, but her heart had pounded for hours. She didn't want to leave because she hadn't accomplished her goal of putting a stop to the Brothers of Sin once and for all.

But maybe the hit on Judge Mason was enough. Maybe Jake was right and these MacKenzies would find the evidence tying them to the crime. And what if her testimony was the final nail in the coffin of the case? Didn't she owe it to Heather to go with Jake, even if she hadn't managed to take down Brandon personally?

Eva scrubbed her hands through her hair in frustration. God, she didn't know what to do. Go with Jake and ruin all her preparation or stay here and take a chance that she could get something more?

She thought of some of the tattoos she'd done today. One of the Brothers came in to have the name of his new baby inked beneath the other names he carried on his skin and another had wanted a swastika. Geez, the contrasts in these people.

It wasn't a surprise in some ways. Everyone was different and even racist criminal assholes had feelings. Too bad those tender feelings didn't extend to all of humankind. The world would be a better place if everyone stopped hating everyone different from them.

The door to her shop burst open and she turned. Brandon Cox looked meaner than usual today and her heart rate kicked up. She hadn't seen him all day, which she counted as a blessing, but he was never far from her mind.

"Here's how it's gonna be, Eva," he said, strutting into the confines of her shop. "I'm tired of you being a prissy bitch. You're gonna spread those pretty legs for me whenever and wherever I want you to. You're gonna suck my dick, and you're gonna be happy about it. No more fucking around. No more focusing on your art bullshit. You can fuck *and* tattoo, and I'm done waiting for you to figure that out."

Her heart hammered as fear and revulsion slid through her. She backed herself against the wall, near her drafting table, frantically trying to think of what to do next.

"You have an old lady, Brandon. You don't want me. I'm nothing compared to her."

He snorted. "That's the thing, baby—Tiffany's gone. Walked right on out of here this morning like her shit don't stink. She ain't coming back."

Oh God. Eva darted her tongue over her lips. Had Tiffany really walked out? Or was she buried in the woods somewhere like Heather had been?

Don't go there.

She couldn't think about that. Just absolutely couldn't. Brandon lunged for her. The overpowering smell of whisky wafted from him as she dodged and put her chair between them.

"You don't want to do this, Brandon."

"Damn sure do."

"You're drunk."

"Not so drunk I can't get it up. Now come here, baby, and give me a kiss."

He made to grab her and she dodged left—but then he changed course, his strong hand wrapping around her upper arm. She threw herself backwards, knocking him off balance just enough to get away. She crashed into her drafting table—then scrambled frantically for her gun. Her fingers closed over the grip just as Brandon wrapped a fist in her hair and yanked.

Eva screamed as the pistol slipped from her fingers and Brandon backhanded her. The momentum knocked her toward the table again and this time she scrambled with both hands to get a hold of her weapon. She spun, raising her gun high as she did so. She was shaking like a leaf, but no way would she miss if she had to pull the trigger. No way.

Brandon staggered to a halt. His face clouded with fury. "Put that fucking thing down, Eva."

Elation washed through her. She finally had Brandon at the end of her weapon, and it felt good. Damn good. "Not happening, asshole. You come near me and I'll shoot."

"Shoot me and your life is over. You got that, bitch?"

She held the gun tightly. "Yes, I understand. But maybe it's worth it to me. You ever think of that?"

"Jesus, you are one crazy bitch. Think that pussy is made of gold or something?"

"No, but I think it's mine. *I* get to decide who I share my body with, not you."

Brandon smirked. "Here's how it's gonna go. I'll walk out of here, but this ain't over. You can count on that, babe."

The door jerked open and Jake loomed in the entry. His gaze shot to her and then over Brandon. Brandon turned sideways, darting looks between her and Jake.

"You believe this crazy bitch? Thinks she's gonna shoot me."

Jake held up both his hands, as if she were aiming at him too. And maybe she was, because he was in the line of sight. But she couldn't put the pistol down. No way.

"Why don't we walk out of here, boss? Leave her to herself for a while."

Brandon shoved a hand through his hair. "Yeah, maybe so."

He turned toward Jake and Eva let out a shaky sigh of relief as he took a step. She lowered the gun—and then Brandon turned and lunged for her, the crazed look on his face screaming for her blood.

She brought the gun up and fired—and Brandon dropped. He roared, clutching his arm and writhing on the floor. Jake leapt on him and knocked him out with a blow, then jumped up and grabbed her hand—but not before disarming her and tucking her weapon into his jeans.

"We have to go, Eva. Right fucking *now*."

* * * *

This was not how he'd intended to do this. Jake hauled Eva out the door and into the yard as the Brothers poured out of the main building in the compound. The gun going off had been loud but they hadn't yet realized where it was or who'd been shot. Jake hoped they would stay confused for a few more minutes.

He yanked Eva around the side of the building and down through the darkened alleyway. She didn't fight him—why would she?—and he picked up the pace. They had to reach his bike, and then they had to bust out of this compound before the rest of the Brothers could organize themselves and figure out what was going on.

When they reached where he'd parked behind one of the buildings, he climbed onto the bike and urged her up behind him. Then he began walking the motorcycle toward the fence. No need to start it until the last second. He'd been intending to cut through the wire at a different location, but he'd also tested the wood and found it was weak in spots. He just had to allow enough room to start the bike and gain the momentum to crash through.

He could hear the roar of confusion and anger out front, and he knew it wouldn't be long before they discovered Brandon knocked out cold and bleeding from a wound to the arm. All hell was going to break loose when they did.

"Hang on," he muttered to Eva.

She clung tightly to him, her scent a lovely cloud of sweetness surrounding him. With a twist of the key, he started the bike. Harleys weren't quiet, but the Brothers were shouting loudly enough in the front yard that they wouldn't hear this one until he revved it and shot for the fence.

"Hey! Who is that? Where are you going?"

Jake didn't bother to look at who was yelling. Instead, he twisted the throttle and the motorcycle raced toward the fence like it had been launched from a slingshot.

Eva screamed as they hit. The fence splintered with a thundering crack and then they were through, racing through a field before they could reach the road about a half a mile away. He prayed there was nothing to stop their progress because if they got stuck in the field they were sitting ducks.

Behind him, he could hear the cacophony of dozens of motorcycles revving up. The Brothers were going out the front gate, but it wouldn't take them long to reach the road running parallel to the compound. He couldn't risk running without lights, not yet anyway, so they could currently see where he was headed. Once out of this field, he'd take countermeasures.

They bounced over a small hillock and the bike went airborne. Eva's grip on him tightened, her body plastering against his as they sailed through the air and hit the ground again hard. And then they were nearing the road and he was turning hard right, the gravel on the roadside spraying the field and road behind them as he hit the throttle. Once on pavement, the ride smoothed out.

When he cut the lights, Eva cried out. But there was no choice. He still knew this road like the back of his hand since he'd ridden it a lot as an angry teenager. Provided they didn't hit a deer, they'd be okay. He hoped.

It was impossible to hear anything over the rush of the wind and the sound of the pipes, but he wasn't taking anything for granted. So far as he was concerned, the Brothers were right behind him.

He'd memorized the coordinates for the safe house, but he couldn't go straight there. First he had to confuse the enemy. It would take some time but it had to be done.

"Turn the lights on," Eva shouted in his ear. "Are you crazy?"

"No chance," he yelled back to her.

Her grip on him tightened as they raced through the night, but she didn't say anything else. When he hit the town limits, he turned the lights on again. He had no doubt they were still being pursued, but the Brothers were a few miles behind.

He spent quite a bit of time winding down side roads and tracking toward the safe house in a roundabout way. It was a couple of hours before they reached their destination, which was a small ranch house tucked into the woods and hidden from view. He'd ridden past it and then doubled back by a different route, and that had added onto their time.

Once, they'd come close to the Brothers. He'd pulled into a driveway and shut off the engine and lights when a group of motorcycles roared by. After they'd disappeared, Jake had carefully eased onto the road and headed down a different street.

There was an outbuilding where he parked the motorcycle. Once he shut it off and everything was quiet, he could hear Eva breathing.

"You okay?"

She snorted. "No. Hell, no. Did I kill him?"

"I'm afraid not."

She cried out and then her forehead thumped against his back. "Fucking hell," she moaned. "All of this and he still isn't dead?"

"No. But it's not over, Eva. There's still Judge Mason and his wife, and you're the key to taking him down over that one. We *will* get him. I promise you that."

"I hope you do. Because someone has to. He's gotten away with too much for too long."

He held his hand over his shoulder so she could take it and dismount first. "Let's get inside."

She climbed down. When her feet hit the ground, he swung a leg over and joined her, his entire body still vibrating from the feel of the bike between his legs.

"I'm hungry," she said. "I hope there's food in the house."

"There will be." Jake found the key where Declan had told him it would be and opened the door. He made Eva stand back as he drew his weapon and cleared house. There was no one inside, so he motioned her in. Then he bolted the door behind them and took out his phone so he could report in to the MacKenzies.

Declan answered on the first ring. When Jake informed him of the situation, the other man blew out a breath. "You made it just in time. Judge Mason died about two hours ago."

CHAPTER SEVEN

Eva stood at the refrigerator, staring inside but not really seeing the food. She was hungry, but she was also sick with worry. Because she'd failed. She'd had Brandon Cox in her sights and she'd failed to kill him. Jake said he wasn't dead. Maybe Jake was wrong...

She closed her eyes. No, Jake wasn't wrong. She'd been scared and she'd aimed poorly. She'd shot Brandon in the arm. If she was lucky, she'd hit an artery and he'd bleed out before anyone could do anything.

She didn't think she was that lucky.

"Hey."

She looked up at the man standing beside her, illuminated by the light from the fridge. Her heart skipped and her belly clenched at the sight of him. He was so gorgeous, and so tough. Not her type. Not at all her type...and yet her body reacted. Strongly.

Her nipples beaded and her skin tingled—and she felt the wetness between her thighs, the aching need there.

"You okay?" he asked, folding his arms over his chest.

"I'm...yeah, I'm okay. Just kind of numb, you know?"

"Yeah, I know." He tipped his chin toward the fridge. "You find anything in there you want?"

She turned back to the contents. "I don't know."

He reached past her and grabbed a package of lunchmeat and some cheese. "Here, let's fix a couple of sandwiches. You get the bread, okay?"

"Sure." She went over to the counter and picked up the loaf of bread, bringing it over to the table where Jake had sat down with the meat, cheese, and some mayonnaise. She sat and he took the bread and opened it up. A few seconds later, she had a sandwich in her hand.

"Take a bite, Eva. Promise it'll taste good."

She did as he said. Somehow, she ate the whole thing, not even aware that she'd done so until she looked up and it was gone.

"Here, have another."

"I can't," she began. But Jake pushed the sandwich on her anyway.

"They're small, and you're in shock. Eat."

She finished the second sandwich while he fixed his. "I've never shot anyone before," she said after a few moments of silence.

He smiled. "I know. But you did good."

She blinked. "What do you mean I did good? I didn't kill him, and I really wanted to."

"Considering the way he startled you, and how scared you already were, it's pretty amazing you hit him at all. Trust me, you did good."

"You'd have killed him if you'd shot him."

"Yes."

"Why didn't you?"

He looked grim for a second. "Those were not my orders.

Besides, getting you out of there alive was more important."

She scrubbed her hands up and down her arms. "Wow, I just can't believe it. Everything I worked for—everything I wanted—it's gone. Over. I'm no longer inside the compound and Brandon Cox is still alive—and free."

Jake reached over and took her hand. She tried not to let his touch affect her, but that was a hopeless endeavor. He definitely affected her.

"The MacKenzies are still working on tracking Snake. But Eva...Judge Mason died tonight. Your testimony is going to be key in putting Brandon behind bars."

A cold feeling of dread washed through her. "What if it's not enough? What if he gets away with it? He always gets away with it." She felt a hot tear escape and she reached up to dash it away angrily.

"Every winning streak has to come to an end. It's time for his to be over—and I'm sure it will be with you, and the power of the MacKenzies, to make it happen."

She sucked in a breath and forced her racing heart to calm. "You trust these MacKenzies, huh? How long have you worked with them?"

His smile was unexpected. "Yeah, I trust them. But I've only worked with them a few days. This isn't my real job."

"It isn't?"

"No. I'm a soldier, Eva. I didn't leave the military, but my skills are what the MacKenzies needed on this job. That and the fact I was once a Brother. I presumably had the best chance of getting inside and getting to you. Didn't know I actually knew you though."

"As if. We had classes together once. You brought my sister home a few times. We didn't know each other."

"No, not in any real way. But I know what I remember about you."

She pushed back from the table and stood, crossing her arms self-defensively. "None of that applies anymore. I'm not Evelyn Collier. She died sometime after Heather, but she died all the same."

"You made yourself over solely to catch Brandon Cox."

"I studied him. Studied them." She shrugged. "It wasn't difficult. Just time consuming." She held out her arms. "These take time. Honing my art took time. Getting their attention and respect took time. I didn't just walk in there with my machines and set up shop."

"Weren't you scared?"

She swallowed. "Hell yeah, I was scared. I went to work in a tattoo shop near The Island—you know the bar they frequent, right?" At his nod she continued. "A couple of them came over, looked at my portfolio, and took a chance. It was just a matter of time after that."

"And somehow you got them to respect your wishes not to touch you. Amazing."

"I think it amused Brandon. I knew it would wear off eventually and he'd come for me, but I hoped to take them down before it happened." She shivered as she thought of Brandon Cox in her shop earlier, demanding that she spread her legs for him.

"Some might consider using your body as simply another facet of the plan."

Her throat tightened. "I couldn't let him touch me. That was a bridge I wasn't willing to cross."

"It's okay, Eva. I wasn't suggesting you should. I'm glad you didn't. Not that it's wrong if that's your thing. But for you it means you have at least a scrap of humanity left inside you. You would do anything to take down Heather's killer—but not that. That was your line in the sand, and it's perfectly okay to have one."

"Do you?"

He rocked back on the chair and studied her. He was so much more than a Brother, wasn't he? This man was one of the good guys. She was more glad for that than she could say. And not just because her life was in his hands.

"Maybe so. Haven't found it yet, though."

There was a noise in the distance that made her pivot. Harleys? She listened hard, then spun back to Jake for a reaction. He hadn't moved an inch.

"Traffic on the road. It's not them, don't worry. If they get close, I'll know it."

She swallowed against the knot in her throat and the butterflies in her belly. "How?"

"There's an alarm system. If anyone trips it, I'll know. We'll have a two-minute warning."

"Is that enough?"

He grinned. "With me? Yeah, plenty."

* * * *

Jake stayed awake long after he convinced Eva to go to bed. There was only one room in this tiny house, but he didn't need to lie in a bed to rest. He'd stretch out on the couch, and he'd listen for the early warning system to go off. He didn't think the Brothers would find them here, but you couldn't ever know how things would go down.

Sometimes the bad guys got intel and they found you. Sometimes they chased themselves in circles until you found them. Except this wasn't a normal operation and he wasn't looking for the Brothers the way he'd stalk terrorists.

He scrubbed a hand over his face, still processing everything that had happened. Jesus, Judge Mason was dead. That wasn't the outcome he'd hoped for, and it pissed him off more than he'd expected. Made him more determined.

He picked up his phone and dialed a number. Cade "Saint" Rodgers, the leader of HOT's Echo Squad, answered on the first ring.

"Harley, been wondering about you, man. How's it going out there?"

His team had been informed about his mission, though not all the particulars of it. Though Colonel Mendez hadn't formally authorized it, they'd told him they were only a phone call away if he needed them.

"It's dicey. Need you to get Hacker researching some stuff." Hacker was Sky Kelley, their computer whiz who hadn't ever met a network he couldn't crack. Jake knew that the MacKenzies were on the job too, but it never hurt to have a little backup.

"What do you need?"

Jake gave him a list of stuff, starting with Brandon Cox and Heather Collier and ending with Snake and the Masons.

"You need us there?" Saint asked, and Jake grinned.

"Nope, I got it. But I appreciate it. Gonna need you when I bring her in though. Pretty sure Cox and the boys will try to get at her. They may seem like a bunch of good old boy redneck bikers, but they've got ties to some bad shit. Organized crime, drug dealers, and sex traffickers. They won't let this go and quietly await their fate."

"You got it, man. See you soon."

"Yep." Jake ended the call and settled back on the couch with his hands behind his head as he stared up at the ceiling. He had a computer, weapons, and the keys to a Mustang that sat behind the house. The first sign of trouble and he was grabbing Eva and bugging out.

But until then, he could lie here and dream about those blue eyes and the way that sexy body had felt pressed against his during the long ride to get here.

CHAPTER EIGHT

Eva couldn't sleep. She kept thinking about that moment when Brandon had meant to rape her and her skin crawled. She'd never been touched by a man. Not like that anyway. Being in the business she was in, she'd certainly been fondled. She'd even been grabbed a time or two, but she'd always dealt with it swiftly and brutally. A kick to the balls did wonders.

Oh, she'd sometimes thought she was going to die for being so difficult. The kind of men she'd spent the last few years around were definitely not the kind to piss off, but she'd done it and she'd survived. Somehow.

She lay in the dark and stared at the ceiling. She'd often wondered if something was wrong with her. She'd never felt desire, not really. She'd never really been on a date or let herself have any sexual feelings toward a man. She'd been too focused on her goals, and no one had interested her.

But then Jake Ryan had crashed back into her life, and her body responded. In spite of her belief that she was dead inside, that desire and love weren't possible, her reaction to him was quite the opposite. She wasn't dead inside. Her body *could* feel desire. It was a shock and a mystery. It was also alarming.

Who was Jake Ryan? He wasn't a Brother anymore, that was for certain. But he wasn't the kind of guy she'd spent the last few years dreaming about either. She'd thought that once she took down the Brothers, once she made Brandon pay for what he'd done, she'd find a nice man and settle down. An accountant. A lawyer. A real estate broker, or even a postman. She didn't care, so long as his life was drama free and she could rely on him not to turn into an adrenaline junkie asshole criminal.

Not that Jake was a criminal. No, he definitely wasn't that. But he *was* a badass and he thrived on danger. That was not what she wanted. Heather had been attracted to badasses and look what that had gotten her.

Eva threw off the covers and sat up. She needed a drink of water. She'd seen bottles in the fridge, so she decided to go and get one. The living room was silent and dark. She padded across the room and opened the refrigerator to snag a bottle. When she turned and started back, a noise from the couch made her squeak in surprise.

Well, where else would he be? This place was only one-bedroom—not that she'd been thinking about that when she went to the kitchen.

"Nice view," Jake said, his voice a throaty growl that made her tingle deep inside.

"I thought you were asleep." She wished he was because she hadn't put her jeans back on. She was standing there in a T-shirt that didn't cover her ass and a pair of sensible cotton panties. They weren't exciting, but they were still panties.

"I was until you walked past."

"I didn't make any noise. I was careful."

"I'm trained to hear a mouse squeak a mile away, Eva."

It was a silly thought, but also a comforting one. "Well, I'm sorry."

He pushed upright. "It's okay. I wasn't sleeping well. You doing all right?"

She hugged herself, as if she could hide her naked legs and the thin panties barely covering her butt as she did so. "Can't sleep."

"I can fix that for you. If you let me."

His voice was so deep and sensual that her nipples beaded tight. "How?" As if she didn't know.

"A good orgasm does wonders."

Her body flushed with heat. "Does it?"

He cocked his head to the side, and she cursed herself for sounding so prissy. Dammit, she might be a virgin, but did she have to sound like one?

"If you don't know, then you haven't been getting any good ones. Or maybe it's been a long time. Has it?"

"You know I didn't let any of the Brothers touch me. So, yeah, it's been a long time. Unless you count the ones I give myself, and then it hasn't been that long."

Oh hell, she was babbling. She swallowed and told herself to zip it.

"You like giving them to yourself?"

"It's the only ones I'm getting, so yeah, I do."

"That's a shame. Let me know if you want to change that. I'm right here."

Her heart pounded. Her skin flushed. A reckless part of her wanted to take him up on it—and yet she couldn't. She had no experience. No ability. She'd embarrass herself if she tried.

He dropped his head into his hands. "Jesus, I'm sorry. Forget I said anything. You just look so damn sexy standing there in your underwear, and it's been a while for me too. But I'm over the line—and after what you've been through, that's unforgivable. You're safe with me, Eva. I'm not like Brandon or any of those assholes."

Her heart thumped. Hard. "What? No, I'm not worried about that. Jake, you've been nothing but decent and kind—" She sucked in a breath as he looked up at her, his gorgeous eyes melting into hers. "It's just, well, I don't know what to do. I don't have the first clue, and that's the truth."

"It's okay, Eva. It's too much too soon. I shouldn't have said anything."

He hadn't understood her. He'd thought she meant she didn't know what decision to make when she literally meant she didn't know what to do.

"No—I mean I don't know. I've never…"

He was frowning. "Never? Never what?"

"Sex. I've never done it."

* * * *

Jake almost couldn't believe what he was hearing out of this gorgeous, kickass woman's mouth. His dick was rock hard, even though he was busy berating himself for it. She didn't need him to come on to her after the night she'd had—and, whoa, she damn sure didn't need it now.

"You're a virgin?"

She shifted on her feet, clearly uncomfortable. "Well…yes. I know that's hard to believe."

It *was* hard to believe—and yet he didn't doubt she was telling him the truth. "I believe you… But why, Eva? Why didn't you ever find anyone you could be with?"

She sighed. "Do you mind if I put some pants on. I can't very well stand here and talk to you this way."

He stood and handed her the blanket he'd been using. "Wrap this around you."

She reached for it and then stepped back as if he might bite, wrapping it around her tightly. "Thanks," she said before opening her water bottle and taking a drink.

"You're welcome."

She sighed. "I don't think it was on purpose, really. It's just..." She seemed to be thinking about her answer. "After Heather died, my mother got sick. It wasn't a sickness that should have killed her, but I think she lost the will to live. Just stayed in bed and wouldn't get out of it except to go to the restroom. She lay there for months, barely eating, refusing to go out. And then one morning she was gone. Just like that. I went to check on her, and she was dead. Her heart gave out."

"I'm sorry, Eva." He didn't know what it was like to lose a parent. He knew what it was not to have any parents in the first place, to be shuttled through the foster care system until you just didn't care about anything anymore. He understood she'd been grief-stricken. He didn't understand how that felt.

"After that, I was alone. Well, my aunt and uncle were still around, but I was eighteen. I kept seeing Brandon Cox and the Brothers ride through town, kept thinking how Mama and Heather would still be alive if not for them—and I made a plan. I decided to turn myself into the kind of woman who could get close to them—and not just close, but someone they would value in their own way. Someone they wouldn't view as a complete outsider. Maybe fucking my way in would have been easier—but I couldn't do it. Every time I thought about it, my skin crawled and I thought I would puke."

"And you were so focused on what you needed to do to get

inside that you didn't spend any time having fun or being yourself."

She nodded. "Yep, that's true. There was no time for dating or men. What was I supposed to do? Date some guy and then disappear when it was time to make my move on the club? That wasn't going to happen. Besides, it takes time to get good at tattooing. I spent years studying with some of the best. I came back to town six months ago and I've been working since."

Jake could only admire her. She stunned him. Eva Gray had the mindset it took to be a Special Ops warrior. Give her some training and focus, and he had no doubt she'd conquer the challenge. That was the kind of single-minded purpose you wanted in an operator. Someone who kept her eyes on the goal and didn't let anything get between her and it.

"Damn, Eva. Who knew all that grit was lurking under those glasses and shy smile of Evelyn's, huh?"

She laughed. "No one, apparently. Not even me. Sometimes I thought it was impossible. But I kept going anyway."

"You said you wanted to be an interior designer at one time. Do you still want to do that?"

She shrugged. "Sure. Maybe. But I like tattooing. I didn't know I would when I started, but I really do. I love doing a tattoo for someone and then they're so stoked to wear it. They go away with my art on their bodies. I love that." She sighed and he heard the sadness in it. "I've lost my portfolio and machines. I can replace the machines and ink—but all the pictures of what I've done, the sketches. I can't replace those."

It wasn't an important thing when lives were at stake—and yet he understood what she must be feeling to lose something valuable to her. "It's not over yet, honey. Don't give up hope."

"It's silly, right? They're just pictures, and this is so much more important. But I feel like my life is in there, like it's the story of me. I guess that doesn't make a lot of sense."

"It makes sense." Because the story of him was told in the missions he'd been on, in the camaraderie with his team, and in the knowledge that he made a difference in this world.

"Thanks for understanding." She unwrapped the blanket from her body and handed it to him. He tried not to look down at her legs, at the dark vee of pubic hair behind her white panties, or the curves of her waist and high mounds of her breasts. Now was not the time for this.

But his dick ached and his gut churned and he wanted so much to reach out and touch her. He wouldn't, but he wanted to.

"I think I should try to sleep now," she said. "Who knows what tomorrow will bring, right?"

In spite of himself, he caught her hand and pressed a kiss to the back of it before letting her go. "You're right. You're also pretty amazing. Get some sleep, beautiful."

She hesitated for a moment—and then she stood on tiptoe and pressed a kiss to his cheek. "You're pretty amazing yourself, Jake Ryan."

She marched into the bedroom, closing the door behind her. He lay down on the couch and pulled the blanket up. The blanket that was now permeated with her scent.

Yeah, it was gonna be a long-ass night.

CHAPTER NINE

"Come on, we've gotta go." A hand shook her shoulder and Eva blinked awake, her heart racing as she realized who it was and what was happening.

"The Brothers?"

"A perimeter breach. Won't take them long to get here, so come on."

Eva scrambled from the bed, grabbing her pants and yanking them on. Then she snatched her boots from the floor and yanked those on too. It took seconds. Jake urged her out the door and through the back of the house to another door. When he opened it, his weapon held at the ready, she strained her ears to hear anything in the darkness.

That's when the deep-throated purr of motorcycles reached her. Jake grabbed her hand and tugged her outside, pushing her toward a car that she hadn't even known was there. He clicked the locks and she got inside while he did the same. When he started the car, the deep growly sound of a high-performance engine vibrated through her.

"What about your Harley?"

His teeth flashed white in the darkness. "Not mine. Belongs to the MacKenzies. They'll get it back eventually."

Jake didn't turn on the headlights, but that was no surprise after the dark ride along the highway earlier. He'd about given her a heart attack then. Now, well, at least this was a car and she felt a little more protected if they ran off the road. Probably just an illusion, but it made her feel marginally better.

"Is there a back way out of here?" she asked as he started driving in a different direction than they'd entered.

"Yes, but I'm going to guess the Brothers are coming at us from both directions."

"How did they find out we were here?"

"They're better connected than you think. There's also a really good possibility they put a tracker on the Harley."

"And you didn't think to look for that?"

"Not all trackers are obvious, Eva. Which means they've got access to some good shit."

She wanted to hyperventilate. "And you people want me to testify against Brandon? What if I don't make it that far?"

Headlights appeared then, coming toward them, and he flexed his hands on the wheel. "You're going to make it. I spend my life fighting these kinds of assholes and I never let the assholes win. It's not in my DNA."

"I used to think you were one of the assholes."

He snorted and revved the engine. "Yeah, well I used to be. Not anymore. Now hang on."

Eva barely had time to brace herself when the car shot forward like a projectile. The seatbelt grabbed her and held her so tightly she couldn't have moved even if she'd wanted to. Jake pointed the car toward the approaching headlights and flat out drove like a demon was on his heels. He glanced up in the rearview and his expression tightened. That's when she knew they were being followed too.

"Are you planning to mow them down?"

"If I have to." He increased the speed and then flipped on the Mustang's lights at the last second. The motorcyclists screeched to a halt. Most of them instinctively got out of the way, but a few stood their ground. Jake twisted the wheel and navigated through them without hitting anyone.

There were angry shouts, and the blast of a pistol. More pistols sounded in the night. Jake shouted, "Get down!"

Eva dropped as well as she could with the seatbelt holding her hard in place. The car hit something, bucking almost violently before settling down and shooting forward again.

A window shattered and Eva screamed.

"Take the wheel," Jake yelled at her over the roar of motorcycles and the plinking of gravel.

She reached for the wheel—thankfully the seatbelt had released its grip on her once the car smoothed out—and steered it while praying no trees or ditches appeared in their path.

Jake turned in his seat and raised his weapon. There was a loud roar as the gun fired again and again. Eva's heart thudded but she kept her eyes on the road and the car pointed straight. Jake sank into the seat and took the wheel from her when he'd used up his magazine, and she fell back against her own seat with her palms sweating and her throat clogging.

Yet a tiny part of her was exhilarated at the excitement, which only served to horrify her. No, she did not want this kind of life. She wanted a nice, quiet, boring professional man. She wanted a home in the suburbs and a kid or two. She wanted to bake cookies and go to PTA meetings and be *normal* for once in her life.

Jake Ryan was not normal. Nothing this man did was normal.

Eva turned in her seat to look behind them. The motorcycles were receding quickly in the distance. She turned around again just as Jake slowed and spun the car sideways and onto the road. When the tires hit pavement rather than dirt and gravel, the car took a quantum leap forward in speed. She could feel the relief rolling through her as they sped down the road.

"Are we safe?"

"For the moment," he told her.

"Where do we go now?"

"I got a place. They won't find us there. No one will."

* * * *

Jake was done playing games with the fucking Brothers of Sin. At the first opportunity, he stopped the car and bought a burner phone. He'd turned his phone off entirely so it couldn't be tracked. When he had the burner up and running, he called Saint and told him what had happened. Saint would inform the MacKenzies and Colonel Mendez.

He'd given Saint his coordinates, but asked he not share them with anyone outside of their team. There could be a leak somewhere along the way and the broader the ripples in the pond got, the more likelihood of the information being compromised.

He drove for hours with Eva asleep beside him, heading north and east toward Virginia and the place he knew Eva would be safe. The day dawned cloudy and wet, with rain falling steadily and making everything seem gloomy. Eva woke and they talked a little bit about the weather and the scenery. She asked where they were going. All he said was "Somewhere safe."

By the time they reached the hunting cabin in the Shenandoah Mountains, it was nearly dark again. He pulled into the garage and shut off the engine. They climbed out and went inside the house. He didn't have to clear it because he knew no one would be there.

Eva stood in the living room looking cold and miserable. It had been warm in Georgia, but coming north where it was rainy, plus driving up into the mountains, had dropped the temperature considerably. It occurred to him that he should have stopped and bought her a coat, but he'd been so focused on getting her here that he hadn't thought about it until now.

He picked up the quilt draped on the back of the couch and handed it to her. She covered herself but he could still see her shiver from time to time.

"I'll make a fire," he said. "It'll be warm soon."

"Thanks. Where are we? Is this a MacKenzie safe house too?"

He looked up from the fireplace and the kindling he was currently stacking to make a fire. "This is mine. A retreat from the world when I need it."

He'd never brought anyone here before. This was his sanctuary, his place to regroup whenever he had time off between missions. It was a couple of hours from DC and HOT, but it might as well be on another planet. Which was precisely what he needed from time to time.

She looked around the room with its warm wood walls and sparse furnishings and he wished it was daylight so she could see the view beyond the tall windows that looked over a valley dotted with candy-colored fall leaves. But she'd see it tomorrow morning so he'd have to be patient.

"It's lovely," she said. "Homey."

"It's not much different from the last place." He continued stacking wood.

"I think you're wrong. It's very different. That place was

sterile." She strolled over to a stack of books on the sofa table and ran her finger over the spines. "This has your personality stamped on it."

"Those are just books, Eva."

She picked one up. "Tying flies? Trout fishing? No, you're interested in these things."

Well, yeah, he was. Fishing was peaceful.

"What are you interested in?" he asked as he finished stacking the wood over the kindling and reached for the lighter he kept on the mantel.

She didn't say anything and when he turned to look at her after lighting the fire, she was biting her lip and blinking. Blinking back tears?

"I don't know," she said on a whisper.

He went over and pulled her into his arms, hugging her tight. He couldn't stop himself from stroking her hair as he tried to comfort her. She didn't fight him. No, she reached around him and hugged him back, enclosing him in the quilt with her.

"You've spent so long training yourself to be the woman you needed to be that you've forgotten the woman you were. But she's in there, Eva. You know she is."

"Yes, she is. I'm just not used to thinking about her anymore."

"Then maybe it's time you start."

CHAPTER TEN

It was time she started. Eva closed her eyes and breathed in the clean scent of the man holding her. He smelled like rain and fresh smoke and leather. He smelled heavenly, and he smelled like home, a feeling she hadn't had in so long that she couldn't really remember what it was like.

Except that she felt safe with him. Happy. Loved.

Loved?

Well, maybe that was taking things a bit far, but no one had held her close in so long that she'd forgotten what this kind of contact felt like. She kept her arms wrapped around him, her cheek against his chest and her eyes closed as she listened to the comforting rhythm of his heart.

She became aware of something else before too long. He was sporting a massive erection that pressed against her belly and made her insides liquefy.

"Sorry," he said roughly as she tilted her head back to look up at him.

"Why?"

His gaze was both hot and troubled at the same time. "I

didn't hug you in order to have sex with you. I'm sorry if I'm making you uncomfortable."

"You aren't." It was true. So true. Far from being uncomfortable, she was feeling heated and achy. She wanted to know what would happen if they took this to the next level. How would she feel then? How would it feel to have him inside her, giving her pleasure?

"Yeah, well, I'm uncomfortable," he said. "Because I'm hard for you but I have to let you go before this gets out of control."

His hands dropped away, but she didn't stop hugging him. "Maybe I want to see you out of control."

His nostrils flared as he stared down at her. "Eva, you don't owe me anything. I did my job when I got you out of there. You don't have to pay me for it."

She let him go and took a step back. Then she dropped the quilt to the couch and reached for the bottom of her T-shirt. She dragged it over her head and dropped it. Jake watched her, the pulse in his throat ticking a bit faster than usual.

She didn't know why, but that made her feel bolder. She flicked open the button on her jeans and toed her boots off at the same time. When she pushed her jeans down her hips, his jaw grew tight. The bulge in his jeans was definitely noticeable now.

"Eva. Jesus."

"I want you to be my first, Jake. You won't hurt me or leave me unsatisfied. I want you to show me how good it can be."

He closed his eyes and swallowed. "You've had a difficult couple of days. Don't make a decision you might regret."

She put her hands on her hips, her temper flaring. "Jake Ryan, stop being a jerk. I don't need you to protect me from myself, okay? Like I told Brandon, I get to decide who I share my body with. And I've decided that it's you." She sucked in a breath.

"And don't you dare try to tell me it's not what you want. I can see plain as day that you do—so stop trying to be noble and show me what I've been missing. I *want* you. I want this. Don't tell me you don't want it too."

His eyes were glittering. "No, I can't tell you that."

"Then strip."

She didn't know what he would do, but then he grinned and shrugged out of his cut. Her mouth went dry as his shirt disappeared. He unbuttoned his jeans but didn't shove them off. Instead, he closed the distance between them and put his hands on her hips, dragging her against his body.

"Gorgeous girl," he said before he dipped his head and took her mouth in a possessive kiss.

Her heart soared and her core grew wetter and hotter than before. Every nerve ending in her body was on fire, sizzling and aching and wanting so much more.

She wrapped her arms around his neck, arched her body into him, and nearly groaned at the feel of bare skin on bare skin. She'd never been this close to a man before. Never known the pure pleasure of that naked touch. Considering she was still wearing her bra and panties, she wondered how intense the pleasure would be when those tiny scraps of cloth were gone too.

She didn't have long to wait to find out. Jake spread his hands over her back, and then her bra snapped open. He tugged it gently from her shoulders as she lifted her arms so he could remove it. And then she was against him again, bare skin to bare skin She moaned with the pleasure of it.

He kissed her long and deep, then swept her up behind the knees and laid her back on the couch, tugging her panties off and dropping them. When he rose above her, his greedy gaze roamed over her body, leaving prickles of heat and longing in its wake.

"Gorgeous," he said. "Fucking gorgeous."

She blushed, because she'd never been naked in front of a man before, never had one look at her like he was a slave to her pleasure. But that's precisely how Jake looked at her—like she was the most important thing in his world at that precise moment and he was going to make sure she got everything she wanted.

He reached out and touched her breasts, his sure fingers flicking her nipples while she bit her lip and moaned softly. Then those clever fingers were sliding down her body to skim over the curls between her legs.

"So many things I want to do to you, Eva. But I think this first time it's important to make sure you're as ready as you can be." He slipped a finger into the seam and found the bud of her clitoris. She gasped as he rolled his finger over her sensitive flesh, sparks bursting behind her eyes. "Think I need to put my mouth here," he said, and the ache of desire grew even more intense.

"Do whatever you want," she gasped. "Just make me come."

His chuckle was deep. "No worries about that, sweetheart. You're going to come several times before I'm finished with you."

She thought he might put his mouth on her, but he took her lips again, kissing her thoroughly and deeply. Then he skimmed his mouth over her jaw, down her throat, finally reaching her nipples. He sucked one and then the other, flicking his tongue over each tight bud while she clutched his head and moaned.

Finally, he made his way down her torso, following the trail of tattoos that she'd once thought were merely cool but now thought were designed to make her body even more sensitive as he traced their loops and curves on the way to his destination.

When he spread her open with his thumbs, she couldn't take her eyes off him. Their gazes met, locking over the pale delta of her body. The firelight bathed them in a warm glow and she thought she'd never seen anything so magical as the sight of Jake Ryan between her legs, his mouth mere inches from her body.

"I want you to remember this night forever," he said gruffly. "Because I'm certain I will, and I don't want to be the only one."

"You won't be."

He lowered his head and licked her, and she nearly came undone right that moment. Never—oh God, *never*—had she imagined it could feel like this. Jake sucked her clit between his lips and she saw stars. There was no way she was going to last, no way she could experience more of this divine pleasure without exploding. She tried to make the orgasm lurking right beneath the surface stay there just a little bit longer, but it was impossible. Jake licked and sucked her, slipped two fingers inside her and curled them against her G-spot, and she exploded with a sharp cry.

He didn't stop licking her and she kept coming until her body shuddered and her breath came out in pants. She opened her eyes to look at him, wondering what she'd see on his face.

What she saw made her heart flip over and emotion well inside her. He looked fierce and pleased at the same time. And he looked possessive. Like he owned her. She hadn't thought she was the kind of woman who would appreciate a man looking at her like that, but oh God, she definitely did.

He produced a condom from his pocket and she blinked. "You were expecting this?" she asked.

"Hoping," he said. "Dreaming. Not expecting." He crawled up her body, his jeans still in place, his hard-on still massive, and kissed her. Tasting herself on his lips made a current of hot possessiveness wash through her. *Mine*, she thought. *He's mine.*

No, it was more like she was his. She didn't know how he felt about any of this, but she knew what she was feeling. And it was a lot more than gratitude or simple desire. Her soul knew his.

Wanted his. They were alike and she felt complete with him. But she had no idea if he felt the same.

"Jake," she breathed as he broke the kiss and tore open the condom wrapper.

"Yeah?"

She rolled her head back and forth on the pillow. "If the rest is anything like that was—well, I may never want to leave this house again."

He shoved his jeans down, freeing his cock, and she drew in a breath at the size and beauty of it. She'd seen cocks before. In porn, a couple of times in person when dudes thought that dropping their pants would make her hot, but she'd never seen one she wanted to explore.

She wanted to touch this one. Taste it. But all of that would have to wait because he rolled on the condom and then picked up one of her legs and wrapped it around him as he positioned himself at her entrance.

"It'll probably be uncomfortable the first time," he said, his amber eyes serious.

"I know." She did know, and she trusted him. He reached between them and rubbed her clit, making little sparks shoot along her nerve endings as her breath caught.

He bent to kiss her and she wrapped her arms around his neck, trying to pull him down to her. And then he pushed forward, his cock stretching her wide as he entered. There was a pinching sensation, a hot sting as flesh tore. A moment later, he was fully inside her.

"You okay?"

She was breathing hard, but only part of that was pain. The rest was excitement and the thrill of making love with this gorgeous man she'd once fantasized about. "Yes."

"It gets better now," he said, flexing his hips and withdrawing a little bit before pushing forward again.

"Oh," she gasped as her body responded to that little bit of pressure. "More. Please, more."

He withdrew again and again, sliding inside her with a little bit of force each time, but not the full force she knew he was capable of. He took her mouth, kissing her hotly as his body possessed hers. Together they climbed toward the peak, their bodies glowing in the firelight, a fine sheen of sweat breaking out on their skin as they moved together. There were sighs and moans and revelations. Jake possessed her completely, loved her delicately hard—if that was a thing—and took her to the edge of something bigger and brighter than she'd ever felt before.

Eva's body tensed as the pleasure spiraled tighter and tighter—and then Jake took her hip in one broad hand and shifted her beneath him, opening her to him even more.

She sailed over the edge as wave after wave of intense pleasure crashed into her senses. Her heart beat hard as hot emotion swelled inside her. She'd lost her virginity, and she was glad for it. After all these years of feeling dead inside, dead to desire or the possibility of ever feeling normal again, she'd been awakened. She wasn't numb. Wasn't broken.

Jake groaned as he found his own release, his hips driving her body down into the cushions of the couch as he pushed deep inside her. His lips sought hers and they kissed for several moments before he broke away and kissed his way to her breasts. He sucked one tight nipple in his mouth while she gasped at how sensitive she was before he pulled away and stood.

She turned on her side as he walked away. He was back a short time later, having dealt with the condom. He climbed onto the couch behind her, scooping her into his body so they pressed together, her back to his front as they watched the fire.

"Any regrets?" he asked her, his breath tickling her ear as he pressed his mouth below it and kissed her neck.

"About you? None at all."

He ran his hand over her hip and then around to cup her sex. "Not quite sure how you feel about this, but I'm thinking this is mine right now."

"For how long?"

"We can start with tonight, but a longer term suits me just fine."

She turned in his arms until she was facing him. The beauty of his face made her belly tighten. "I don't know what any of this means, but I know I feel things for you I haven't felt before. I trust you, and I feel safe with you. But…"

She didn't know what to say. But she didn't need to say anything. He knew.

He kissed her softly. "I scare you because I'm not what you envisioned, right? I imagine you've spent so much time with violent men that you decided you wanted a man who'd never committed an act of violence in his life—and never would."

She dropped her lashes. "That's right."

"I'm not gonna lie, Eva. I've committed violence. I've killed men—but I do it for the right reasons. I'm not a criminal, and I'm not the man I was seven years ago. I fight for freedom, for my country, for the rights our founding fathers granted us when they made this great nation. I fight for justice, and I don't give a good goddamn what color someone is or who they love so long as they're good people and don't commit crimes or acts of terrorism. I won't stop fighting for my country or to protect the people in it, so if that kind of violence is still too much for you, I understand."

Eva gazed up at him, at eyes that made her melt inside, and

knew she'd never find another man who made her feel this way. Jake Ryan was worth more than all the accountants and lawyers in the world to her. A safe man wasn't a man who held a safe job—it was a man with inviolable principles who would do anything to keep you safe from harm when you needed it.

"Maybe you aren't the kind of man I thought I wanted...but you're the kind of man I need. I don't know what this is or where it's going, but I want to find out."

He cupped her ass in his hands and pulled her against a burgeoning erection. "I can tell you where it's going right now, baby, if you think you're up for it again."

She threw a leg over his hip and pressed herself closer. "I think that's a *great* idea..."

CHAPTER ELEVEN

They spent two days in his cabin in the mountains while the MacKenzies and HOT worked to track down Snake and the evidence needed to put Brandon Cox away once and for all. They spent a lot of time naked, but Jake had the presence of mind to take Eva into town for a jacket and some clothing.

They ate simply—for dinner they had cheeses and fresh bread, olive oil for dipping, slices of salami and ham, and fresh veggies. Breakfast was eggs and bacon. Once, Eva made a homemade pizza, tossing the dough and layering the pie with cheese and ham and mushrooms. They'd eaten it on the deck with wine and a view, and then made love by the fire. Perfection.

Jake loved to watch Eva move, whether it was cooking or drawing or simply standing on the deck with her coffee and staring out at the trees while her breath frosted in the air around her. She was graceful and beautiful, and her body was a work of art. Not only because she was shapely and had all the parts he enjoyed most, but her tattoos also enhanced her beauty. They were a vital part of her, telling her story on her skin in black and gray ink.

She had her sister's name on her ribcage, inked with angel wings and roses and stylized loops and curls. He shuddered to think of Brandon seeing that, though probably he'd have never realized the connection since there was no last name.

Eva learned quickly when it came to sex. She'd been sore and they'd had to get creative, but she was enthusiastic about whatever they tried. Jake loved being buried inside her, loved seeing the sensuality and wonder in her eyes as he brought her to orgasm. He loved women and loved sex, but he'd never craved a woman's pleasure the way he did this one's. There was nothing he wanted more than to see her wrapped around his cock and shuddering in bliss.

It began to dawn on him the more he touched her that he didn't want to touch anyone else. That Eva Gray had somehow become *the* woman for him. He hadn't been looking—hadn't wanted to settle down with anyone—but here she was and all he could think about was keeping her safe. Coming home to her at the end of a mission and losing himself in her arms.

It was disconcerting as fuck, especially for a man like him. He'd spent a lifetime making sure he didn't need anyone, and this one woman had turned his life upside down in a matter of days.

When his burner phone rang, he knew their time in the cabin was at an end. He answered with a clipped "Ryan." Saint was on the other end.

"Need you to bring her in. Hacker and Cypher have found Snake, aka Darrell McKeown, and he's being picked up as we speak. Also, and this is the really important one for your girl, Tiffany Jenkins's body was found yesterday by hunters. Beat up, shallow grave, same M.O. as Heather Collier. If we can get one of the Brothers to crack, we'll have Brandon Cox on the murder of his girlfriend, too."

"Don't count on it," Jake growled, his gut churning with anger. Could he have saved Tiffany? Should he have realized what was happening and done something? But there'd been nothing to indicate what Brandon was about to do. Hell, he'd been fucking Tiffany in his room the night of the bonfire and she'd come out looking dreamy and satisfied, so they hadn't been fighting. She'd had no bruises, no marks of any kind that he could remember.

Fuck.

"Yeah, well, we'll see. Between Snake, and Eva's testimony, think we can rattle the club enough to break when they see where things are going. Someone will squeal to save his ass."

"What about the other ties? Find anything on who they're dealing with in the crime world?"

"Hacker's working on it with Cypher. Think they'll get it cracked before too long."

"Gonna need heavy security for Eva. She's a high-value target to Cox and the Brothers right now—and to whomever they're dealing with since ending the Brothers creates problems for their business partners."

"Well aware, mi amigo," Saint said. "Cox is still free for the moment, but soon as we have Eva's statement and we can crack Snake, this will be over. Bring her to DC. This is a federal case so the fibbies will have to take the statement, but she'll have protection until Cox is taken into custody."

"Copy that. On the way."

* * * *

Eva had never been to Washington, DC, before. She'd been to Atlanta plenty of times, and to Dallas and a few other cities, so the traffic wasn't necessarily a surprise. Seeing the monuments she'd only ever seen in pictures and on television was pretty surreal, however. Things were never quite the way you thought they were. For one thing, the distance between the Lincoln Memorial and the capitol was a lot farther than it looked in pictures. Not that she had a chance to walk it, but Jake drove her through the city so she could see as much as possible.

He took her to a building out in the suburbs that was surrounded by razor wire and security cameras. She met with an FBI agent and gave her statement while Jake sat in a chair beside her and didn't say anything. Another agent came in and they questioned her endlessly about what she'd heard, what she'd seen, and what she might know that she'd forgotten.

She told them everything she knew and when it was over, when she was exhausted from the ordeal, Jake took her to a hotel. She'd thought they'd be alone, but she realized as she got out of the car that another car had followed them. A group of men she didn't recognize emerged. She shot a glance at Jake but he didn't look alarmed. Instead, he grinned as the men swaggered over.

"Harley, it's good to see you again," one of the men said.

"Saint." Jake and the man did the bro-hug thing and then the others started talking and slapping backs too. When it was over, Jake stepped back and took her hand, tugging her into the curve of his body.

"Guys, this is Eva. Eva, this is my team—Cade, Mal, Ryder, and Noah. We've got others, but they're off doing business for us elsewhere."

Eva greeted them all. She'd never remember names, but they were all tall and muscled. Dangerous men, every one of them. Except these didn't make her skin crawl. That's because, if they were anything like Jake, they were solid down to their core. The kind of men you wanted at your back in a fight.

"Ma'am, we've got to keep you safe until we know Brandon

Cox is in custody," the one named Cade—whom Jake had also called Saint—said.

"What's the word from Declan MacKenzie?" Jake asked.

"They're ready to go in with the fibbies." He looked at his watch. "I imagine it's happening right now."

Now that the FBI had her statement, he meant. Her pulse skipped along as a spike of fear rolled through her but Jake squeezed her hand and she felt calm wash over her. She had him, and that was all she needed.

They ushered her into a hotel suite and the men set up a command center. No one was getting in or out without going through them, and that made her feel somewhat better.

She was standing by the window, looking out at the surrounding landscape and the distant dome of the capitol, when Jake walked into the bedroom area to join her.

"You doing okay?"

She shrugged. "I'm fine. Tired, but fine."

He came over and wrapped his arms around her, tucking her head beneath his chin and just holding her. A wave of happiness flowed through her. She loved this man. So quickly, so completely. She hadn't said the words yet, though. She didn't know if he felt the same way, or if she was floating along in a sea of delusion. Just because the sex was hot and the emotion seemed so intense between them didn't mean he was in love with her.

"You're pretty amazing, Eva. You did a good job today. They're going to get Brandon."

"I hope so...but I still feel like I failed Heather. He may go down, but he won't ever admit to killing her."

Jake had told her about Tiffany. She'd felt a blow of grief hit her, not because of Tiffany, though she hadn't wished the woman any harm, but because it had brought back all the pain and anguish from the day they'd gotten the news about Heather. Life had changed that day, and it never changed back again. She'd wanted to get revenge, but she didn't feel like she had. It was hollow, even if there was victory.

"I know, baby," Jake said, running his hands up and down her back. "I know."

There was a knock on the door a few minutes later. "Come in," Jake said but he didn't let her go.

It was Cade. "It's done. They've stormed the compound and taken everyone into custody. They'll be processed. Most will wind up on the streets again, but Brandon and the leadership will be held until the trial for the premeditated murders of Judge Mason and his wife."

"And Snake?"

"He cracked. Just got word from the MacKenzies. Oh, and something else you should know...there's another informer."

Eva perked up at that news. One of the old ladies? She'd never even suspected. "Who?" she asked as her mind raced over the possibilities.

Cade smiled. "According to Declan, an old guy named Duke. He started talking the instant they raided the place and he hasn't shut up since."

Eva's eyes widened. She met Jake's gaze. "Was he there seven years ago?"

Jake smiled. "He was. If he knows anything about Heather, it's gonna come out. Holy shit, old Duke. Who'd have guessed he'd turn?"

Maybe it wasn't as much a surprise as Jake thought. "He talked about a grandson sometimes when he was in my chair. A boy who lives in Alabama with his mother. Duke went to visit sometimes. He loves that kid a lot. Maybe the thought of going away and never seeing him again loosened his tongue?"

"Maybe so. Or maybe he just got decent with age. It happens. I'm proof of that."

Eva hugged him hard. "You're the most decent person I know. I love you, Jake Ryan."

"Whoa, just gonna leave you two…" Cade said. "Uh, yeah." He turned and slipped back through the door, shutting it behind him.

Jake blinked down at her. "You love me?"

She nodded shyly. Heat suffused her cheeks, but it was too late to back out now. She'd said it.

"Well damn, dreams really do come true. I love you too, Eva Gray. So fucking much."

He kissed her so tenderly that she wanted to weep. She'd spent the past seven years feeling empty and angry and now she had this. Him. Love and happiness and a future to look forward to rather than fear. Life didn't always take you in the direction you thought you wanted to go. Sometimes it took you where you needed to be. And it was so much better than you could have ever dreamed.

CHAPTER TWELVE

One year later…

Eva rolled over in bed and watched her husband approaching with a breakfast tray. They'd gotten married yesterday after a year of living together and loving and being best friends. She couldn't have gotten through this past year without him.

She'd moved to DC and gone to work in a tattoo parlor. Her portfolio and machines had been returned to her after the FBI raided the Brothers of Sin compound, so she hadn't lost her work after all. She'd spent a few months working for someone else before opening her own shop.

Jake's job took him away from home, but he always came back to her. They'd bought a house and moved to a nicer neighborhood. She had the picket fence and the two-car garage, but her fiancé, now husband, was a tattooed badass—she'd added to the tattoos on his sexy body, and she'd even managed to cover the Brothers of Sin tattoo with something better—who cracked heads for a living. And she was a tattooed woman who liked badassery and shooting high-powered weaponry in her leisure time instead of baking cookies and attending neighborhood association meetings.

It hadn't all been perfect, though. She'd had to face Brandon Cox in federal court and testify against him. He'd glared at her with such hate in his eyes that she'd had nightmares for weeks. But there was nothing he could do. He was a toothless lion. His brothers had turned on him. His business partners had abandoned him. The remaining Brothers of Sin had gotten rid of all the illegal activities and were busy working on being legitimate.

Best of all, Brandon had finally been prosecuted for Heather's murder. He'd been found guilty, too, though he'd also been found guilty of murdering Tiffany and hiring the murders of Judge Mason and his wife. Eva had cried like a baby when the verdict for Heather's murder had come down, and she'd wished her mother was still alive to witness it. She'd even gone to visit her aunt, who'd been both shocked and thrilled to see her after so long. Eva had thought no one cared that she'd disappeared, but her aunt had cried and railed at her for never sending postcards or picking up a phone.

They'd worked it out, though, and she stayed in touch on social media and through frequent phone calls.

"Got an envelope for you," Jake said as he set the tray with bacon, eggs, and toast down. The fragrant smell of the coffee made her mouth water. She picked it up and took a sip as Jake handed her the envelope.

She turned it over in her hand. There was a spidery crawl of handwriting on it, but no name, just an address. She slipped it open and pulled out a card. A picture fell out too and she picked it up. A young boy hugged a rugged old man with tattoos and a bandanna and motorcycle leathers.

"It's Duke. How'd he know where to send this?"

Jake shrugged. "I may have let him know where to send it. But don't worry, it's just a PO box."

She opened the card and read what it said.

Dear Eva,

Thank you for the tattoos you did for me. Sorry about your sister. Wish I'd had the guts to say something sooner. I wasn't there when he killed her, but I knew he'd done it when he needed us to lie for him. I went along with it because it's what I knew. I have no excuses, but I want you to know this little boy right here made me want to be a better man. And so I am, with help from God, every day. Bless you and congratulations on your wedding.

Duke

"Wow," she said, handing the card to Jake even while she teared up. "Guess you can never be too sure about anyone, huh?"

"You can be sure about us."

"Yes, I definitely can. You're the best thing that ever happened to me, Jake."

"Don't say stuff like that when your eggs are waiting."

"Why not?"

"Because they'll get cold when I bury myself inside you and make you scream my name instead of eating them while they're hot."

Eva grinned. "Maybe I want to scream your name. You ever think of that?"

His answering grin was wickedly hot. "That's what I hope for every fucking day of my life."

"We can heat the eggs up later."

"That's my girl," he said, moving the tray to the floor and

attacking her body with all the delicious moves he had in his arsenal.

Life with Jake Ryan was never going to be dull. And that's exactly the way she wanted it.

THE END

DISCOVER THE LILIANA HART MACKENZIE FAMILY COLLECTION

Go to www.1001DarkNights.com for more information

Spies & Stilettos by Liliana Hart
Trouble Maker by Liliana Hart
Rush by Robin Covington
Never Surrender by Kaylea Cross
Avenged by Jay Crownover
Bullet Proof by Avery Flynn
Delta: Rescue by Cristin Harber
Hot Witness by Lynn Rayc Harris
Deep Trouble by Kimberly Kincaid
Wicked Hot by Gennita Low
Desire & Ice by Christopher Rice
Hollow Point by Lili St. Germain

DISCOVER THE WORLD OF 1001 DARK NIGHTS

Go to www.1001DarkNights.com for more information

Collection One

Collection Two

Collection Three

Collection Four

Bundles

Discovery Authors

Blue Box Specials

Rising Storm

Liliana Hart's MacKenzie Family

ABOUT LYNN RAYE HARRIS

Lynn Raye Harris is the *New York Times* and *USA Today* bestselling author of the HOSTILE OPERATIONS TEAM SERIES of military romances as well as 20 books for Harlequin Presents. A former finalist for the Romance Writers of America's Golden Heart Award and the National Readers Choice Award, Lynn lives in Alabama with her handsome former-military husband, two crazy cats, and one spoiled American Saddlebred horse. Lynn's books have been called "exceptional and emotional," "intense," and "sizzling." Lynn's books have sold over 3 million copies worldwide.

Lynn loves to hear from readers!

To get in touch with Lynn, send an email to lynn@lynnrayeharris.com.

HOT ADDICTION
Hostile Operations Team, Book 10
By Lynn Raye Harris

Coming April 11, 2017! The explosive NEW story in the Hostile Operations Team series! Dex "Double Dee" Davidson first made his appearance in HOT REBEL, Book 6 of the series. Now he gets his own story!

* * * *

Five years ago…

Dexter Davidson checked his watch for the thousandth time that morning. It was nearing noon and his bride-to-be was over an hour late. His father stood in the chancel, his rented tuxedo making him appear distinguished and genteel rather than rough and worn like the farmer he was. But the look on his face was what killed Dex the most. It was one of pity and a growing resignation.

"Fuck this," Dex growled as he clenched his jaw tight and walked down the aisle, between the rows of pews where the guests waited for the ceremony to start. The chapel doors were open to the outside because it was springtime and warm. But it was also raining. A soft, gentle rain, but rain nonetheless.

Perhaps the rain had caused a delay. Dex stood in the open door and took his phone from his pocket. Annabelle still hadn't answered his texts. He sent another one, just in case, and felt his heart shrivel just a little bit more when no answer came.

He tried calling but it went to voicemail without even ringing. "Belle," he said, his throat tight and his eyes stinging, "where are you, baby? I'm worried. Please let me know you're safe. If you've changed your mind, it's okay. Just let me know."

It wasn't okay if she'd changed her mind, but what else could he say? Annabelle Quinn had been his girl for the past four years. He'd fallen madly in love with her in an instant. He'd known her most of his life, had ignored her for much of it because she was his little sister's best friend, but one day, *pow!*, she'd smiled at him the way she had a million times before—and he was done for. He'd been hers from that moment forward.

And now they were supposed to be getting married. He'd come home on leave from the Army at Christmas and asked her to marry him. She'd said yes. She and his sister had planned everything while he went back to Afghanistan and did his best to stay alive. He didn't know how long he stood there before he felt a presence beside him.

"I'm sorry, Dex." Katie put a hand on his arm. "She's not coming."

He wanted to deny it, but the look on Katie's face told him all he needed to know. He felt hollow inside. Empty. Because he knew she was right. He'd known it for a while now.

His sister's eyes were shiny. He took the phone from her hand and stared at the text message on the screen until the words blurred together and his heart burned away, turning to ash.

Belle*: I can't, Katie. Please don't hate me, but I can't. Tell Dex I'm sorry. I shouldn't have let it go this far. I've thought for a while that marrying him wasn't right, that I'm not the woman for him—I should have been brave enough to say so. He deserves more than this. Tell him.*

Dex stood there for a long moment, his gut roiling with emotions he didn't know how to process. He dropped the phone and strode out into the rain while Kate called after him. He put his uniform hat on, shoved his hands into his pockets, and kept walking down the muddy road. Away from the country church that Annabelle had insisted was the place she wanted to be married.

He didn't know where he was going or what he was going to do when he got there. All he knew was that his life would never be the same again.

ON BEHALF OF 1001 DARK NIGHTS,

Liz Berry and M.J. Rose would like to thank ~

Liliana Hart
Scott Silverii
Steve Berry
Doug Scofield
Kim Guidroz
Jillian Stein
InkSlinger PR
Asha Hossain
Fedora Chen
Kasi Alexander
Pamela Jamison
Chris Graham
Jessica Johns
Dylan Stockton
and Simon Lipskar

Made in the USA
Middletown, DE
26 November 2017